I0551795

CANCER, COVID, & CROCODILES

Ian Bradley

Bradley & Lucas Publications | Sydney

For Mary and Peter
(You know why)

CONTENTS

He survived the three Big Cs,
But he forgot about the Bs.

CHAPTER ONE

Mike Maguire sat in the waiting room of the Radiology unit at the Mater hospital in North Sydney, only vaguely aware of his surroundings. He had been attending the unit for over five weeks of a six-week, five-day-a-week course of radiation therapy, following a full year's hormone and then brachial treatment for prostate cancer.

He wasn't a good patient. Not good, he told himself, because he wasn't used to it. For over fifty years he'd had no reason to go anywhere near a hospital. He only ever saw a doctor when his wife, Mary, bullied him every few years or so to have a check-up, and he never saw a dentist because his teeth were perfect. Then, suddenly, wham! His Prostate Specific Antigen (PSA) reading shot up through the roof and he was hurled into a world of biopsies, MRI scans, invasive examinations, the smell of disinfectant and the smell of death.

The truth is he wouldn't even have had a PSA test if his wife hadn't (again) bullied him into it. It started just before his fifty-fourth birthday when a strange package arrived from the Government like some deranged person's idea of a birthday present.

It was a Bowel Cancer test, recommended for everybody from fifty to seventy-four. Mike looked at the instructions, which involved placing a water-soluble membrane over the toilet bowl while he defecated, then taking a smear from the faeces and sending it off to the Government for testing.

Mike tossed the kit into the rubbish, only to have Mary recover it. She said he was selfish not to take the test. He had a wife, a son, a grandson; he owed it to them to stay well. He should take the test and while he was at it, he should see a doctor and get checked for prostate cancer.

Mike had heard a lot of men joking about being checked for prostate cancer; having some stranger stick his finger up your bum. Well, Mike wasn't having that. He'd have a blood test, but that was it.

If only he'd known.

In the succeeding months he became so used to people, male and female, sticking fingers up his bum, that in the end he just closed his eyes and wished it would all go away. Of course, it didn't and he developed an irrational irritation with Mary for making him take the test. If she hadn't, he would still be blissfully unaware there was anything wrong with him. He would, as Mary pointed out, also be dead, and knowing this may be true, made him even more irritated.

In fact, Mike wasn't sure which irritated him more; his wife's over dramatization or his sister-in-law Valerie's complete indifference. She had practically scoffed when she heard he had prostate cancer.

"Prostate cancer's nothing," she had declared with all the confidence of one who didn't have a prostate. "My father died with prostate cancer and he was ninety-two"

Mike didn't exactly hate his sister-in-law. He was too lazy to hate anybody. But he did dislike her intensely. It wasn't so much the English Finishing School accent as her conviction that only her problems were important.

"Died *with* prostate cancer, not *from* it," he had said, trying to hold his temper, "I'd be happy to die *with* it and if

I made ninety-two, I'd be even happier."

"You probably will," replied his sister-in-law, with more than a hint of regret in her voice.

Mike knew that most men do die with prostate cancer, not from it. They contract the disease so late in life, and it is so slow developing, that treatment is a waste of time and money because they will be dead long before the cancer kills them. But he was barely fifty-four and his cancer was so virulent that there was no chance of him living long enough to die of old age. Little chance of him even reaching sixty.

After a biopsy and a particularly invasive exploratory examination, the Oncologist had told him, shortly after removing his finger from his rectum, that if Mike didn't have treatment immediately, he had only a twenty-three percent chance of surviving the next three years. His only hope was surgery or a cocktail of treatments including an injection of hormones to halt the production of testosterone and shrink the cancer sufficiently for a Surgeon to insert nearly a dozen tubes into his prostate, through which the Oncologist could then blast high dosage radiation directly into the cancers.

Even after nearly a year of hormone treatment the cancers were still so large and widespread that they needed more tubes than the machine could provide with bursts of radiation at any one time. So the process had to be repeated a second time on each of the days he'd been in hospital, where he lay with an epidural rendering him immobile from the waist down while a sequence of jolly Irish nurses poked about at his shrunken nether regions and kept up a constant conversation about anything but prostate cancer.

Neither the Oncologist nor his Surgeon ever told Mike

what treatment he should receive. They simply provided him with a book of statistics predicting his chances of survival based on case histories world-wide. Then they left him to choose his own treatment between hormone therapy, surgery, brachia, radiology or a combination of any two or more of the above. They said there were no bad options; it was up to him.

Obviously, there were bad options, as Mike learnt when he studied the death rates in the book. It was clear to him that the Oncologist and the Surgeon were afraid to make a decision in case they got it wrong and Mike sued them. Or, even worse, he died and his wife sued them. So, they simply gave him the book on survival rates, or more accurately, fatality rates, for cancer patients with varying types and degrees of prostate cancer and told him to make up his own mind.

Mike didn't mind making up his own mind. It gave him the illusion of at least a little control over a process that he had no control over at all. And after his stay in hospital, he drove himself to radiotherapy each morning for the same reason; an illusion of control. Even though, on some mornings, he was almost too tired to keep his eyes open.

All of the other patients in the radiology waiting room, mostly men seemingly years older than Mike were driven to the hospital by their wives. In truth they probably weren't much older than Mike; they were just beaten down by the process. Not only did their wives drive them to radiology, they discussed their cases with their doctors, talked to their nurses, their radiologists, and even the other wives; broadcasting to the world in loud voices the details of their husbands' condition, their loss of musculature, their lack of energy, their loss of libido, and their impotence. Mike would have rather died than hear his wife talk about him like that. So he drove himself to hospital each morning, barely awake and heedless of the fact that he might kill himself. Hence his semiconscious state when the nurse called out his name:

"Mr Maguire?"

Mike was vaguely aware of a man crossing to the nurse. He looked familiar but Mike didn't think he knew him. He was about Mike's age or a little younger: around fifty, but he wore his hair long and his beard ragged. He looked like a 70s hippie but he was too young to have ever been one.

It was while the nurse was talking to the man that it dawned on Mike that the man looked rather like him. Not that Mike would ever wear a beard and a ponytail but the man was the same height, the same colouring. And he had the Maguire look, as Mike's wife Mary would have described it; a look that always made him appear slightly annoyed with the world.

And the similarities didn't end there, as Mike realised when the nurse walked over to him.

"Mr. Maguire?" she enquired, "Mr. *Michael* Maguire?"

Mike nodded.

"The call was for you," she smiled, "Not Mr. John Maguire."

Mike looked at the other man as his resumed his seat. He was seemingly unaffected by the confusion or the coincidence. He didn't even look up as Mike followed the nurse through to radiology.

CHAPTER TWO

As he lay on the radiology bench with a giant ray gun prescribing an arc across his lower abdomen, hopefully killing any cancer cells that might have escaped the brachia treatment, and certainly killing countless healthy cells and rendering him impotent in the process, Mike thought about the man in the waiting room. Could he be a relative? It seemed unlikely; impossible, even.

Mike's father Paddy, as he had been so fond of telling his sons when he was still alive, was one of the countless stolen children after World War II who had been gathered from the orphanages of Great Britain and shipped to Australia under the tender care of various religious orders. But not for Paddy the abuse that befell many of the stolen children, he told them. He arrived at the front gates of the children's home in rural New South Wales, he said, walked straight through the complex, scaled the back wall and hitched a ride to the Snowy Mountains, where he quickly got a job working on the Snowy Mountains hydro-electric scheme.

The workers on the scheme were mostly battle-hardened veterans from World War II but despite his youth Paddy fitted right in. So much so that by the time the hydro-electric scheme was finished, he had amassed a small fortune and moved to Sydney to start his own construction company; cashing in on the boom as Sydney spread out to the suburbs by building simple houses on quarter-acre blocks to accommodate the thousands of migrants from Europe arriving by the boatload, and later by the plane load.

Paddy had no qualifications, but he always said you didn't need qualifications: it was easier to buy people who had them. In fact, he appeared to revel in his lack of education. He despised education. If it wasn't for their mother and the free tertiary education introduced by the Labour Government in the seventies, neither Mike nor his older brother Rory would have gone to university.

What good was a degree anyway? Neither of them had been as successful as their father. Rory had somehow managed to make a failure of his career as a stockbroker, finding himself sued by several of his clients, before escaping to northern New South Wales where he ran the macadamia plantation his father had established as a tax scheme in the eighties.

Mike himself had become a teacher; a good one too, although he always dreamt of writing a novel. He never had the time, or so he told himself. Now he had nothing but time and he still wasn't writing.

Their father regarded Mike and Rory as failures. To Paddy the only measure of success was how much money you had when you died. And Paddy had a lot of money. Even in death he wasn't keen to give it up. Instead, his money was placed in a trust until only one of his sons survived, when he would inherit everything. It was a situation Paddy knew would start a legal battle between the surviving son and his brother's widow; a prospect he relished even from the grave.

In fact, the battle started long before either of the brothers had died. Mike's older brother Rory proposed that they challenge the will while they were still young enough to enjoy the proceeds. The problem was that neither brother could agree on how the fortune would be split. Rory, egged on by Valerie, argued that being the elder son, he should be entitled to the larger share. Mike countered that since he was the younger and statistically the more likely to outlive his brother, *he* should have the larger share; although in reality he was quite prepared to settle for a fifty-fifty split.

Rory and Valerie were having none of it.

The argument was practically the only topic of conversation whenever the family met until Mike announced that he had cancer. Then Rory and Valerie stopped mentioning the will and silently prayed that if the cancer didn't kill Mike, the treatment would.

Mike knew precisely why Rory and Valerie stopped mentioning The Will, and although he was sure the new Maguire in the waiting room, John Maguire, wasn't a long-lost brother, he thought he'd mention it to Rory just to cause trouble. The possibility of somebody else contesting the will would no doubt drive him to distraction.

But then Mike fell asleep on the radiology table and by the time he woke up he'd forgotten all about John Maguire and the will. He wasn't to remember him again until a visit to the family macadamia farm reignited the fight between Mike and his brother; or more precisely between Mike and his sister-in-law, Valerie.

CHAPTER THREE

A
t the end of his course of radiation treatment the Oncologist took Mike into a pokey little office and explained to him that they wouldn't know for months, maybe even years, whether the treatment had been successful. He wanted Mike to go back on the hormone therapy for another year, 'Just in case'; this, despite the fact that, over a year earlier, the Oncologist had told Mike that the hormone treatment would destroy ten per cent of his bone mass every year. After nearly two years of treatment Mike couldn't stand the prospect. Nor did he understand the reasoning behind the request. The hormone treatment cut off Mike's production of testosterone, which the cancer needed to feed on. Mike's testosterone reading was virtually nil. If he wasn't producing any testosterone why did he need hormone treatment to stop its production? He suspected that he was being used as a guinea pig and he didn't like it.

"Do I really have to go on hormones for another year?" he asked.

"You don't *have* to do anything," was the reply.

"Good," said Mike. "In that case I won't bother." And he walked out, vowing never to return.

In due course the Oncologist communicated with the Surgeon and with Mike's GP, a sensible woman called Cathie. Cathie showed Mike a copy of the letter that the Oncologist had sent to the Surgeon and which the Surgeon had passed on to her with his notes scribbled in the margin, rather than bother with another letter. The Oncologist had reported that Mike was querying the need for further hormone treatment when he wasn't producing testosterone. The Surgeon had prescribed a bold circle with his Waterman fountain pen around this section and written in the margin, in even bolder letters '*Bloody good question!*'

Mike saw this as vindication. Mary did not. She worried that he was going against the advice of his oncologist. Mary had a huge fear of disregarding medical advice. Her own father had died more than thirty years earlier and Mary still blamed herself for letting him die.

At about the same age as Mike was now, Mary's father had suddenly started suffering a loss of appetite and a loss of weight. He claimed that he was getting fitter but that didn't explain his lower back pain or what seemed to Mary to be a definite yellowing of his skin and the whites of his eyes. Mary was away at Teachers' College at the time, so she missed some of his decline. On the other hand, it meant that when she did get home, the changes were even more obvious. She urged her father to see a doctor. He refused. Eventually, when he was gripped by a sudden bout of back pain, she had called an ambulance.

Still refusing to admit there was anything wrong with him, her father was nonetheless carted off to hospital, and examined. Even the overworked, inexperienced intern in A&E recognised that he was really ill and immediately suspected that it was cancer.

It was. Liver cancer. Within six months, Mary's father was dead.

They say women marry their fathers and in Mary's case there was an element of truth in that. Mike and Mary's father had a lot in common; in personality and in health. They were both apparently easy going and charming.

And they both seemed to enjoy perfect health; until they didn't. They both refused, or rather simply omitted, to have regular health checks.

The difference was that, having seen her father die, Mary had refused to allow Mike to let things slide. She insisted, as she felt she should have done with her father, that he take tests even when there were no symptoms. Her actions had undoubtedly saved his life. Not that he would admit it. He considered that he had beaten the Big C himself: A fact he was eager to impress on his brother and his sister-in-law, when they invited him and Mary up to the farm *'to recuperate after Mike's terrible ordeal.'*

Of course, they all knew that Rory and Valerie had invited Mike and Mary up to the farm in the hope of hearing that Mike's cancer treatment had failed. Mike was determined to disappoint them, even if the Oncologist had said that they wouldn't know for several years whether the treatment had been successful or not.

"My PSA is zero," he announced, well into the second bottle of wine at dinner, "You can't get any lower than that."

He stared at his brother with a rather malicious grin.

"What's your PSA, Rory?"

"I don't know," muttered Rory.

"You should get it checked." said Mike, "Mind you, I can understand why you don't want to. Those bloody oncologists. Once they've got their hooks into you, they just don't want to let go. I'm sure half the treatments I've had were unnecessary."

"Why would they give you unnecessary treatments?" scoffed Mary, not happy at the way the conversation was going.

"For the statistics," said Mike.

He turned to Rory to explain.

"They have this network all over the world where they exchange their patients' results. They send their patients' records to each other to build up a data bank. They've no idea what they're doing. It's all just trial and error. They just keep trying things until something works."

"Nonsense" said Mary, "You're only saying that because the oncologist wanted you to have another hormone injection."

"Precisely," said Mike.

He again turned to Rory.

"My testosterone level is zero and the oncologist wants to give me hormones to prevent me producing testosterone," he said.

"He just wants to be certain," said Mary.

"He just wants to use me as a guinea pig," said Mike.

There was an uneasy silence.

Valerie smiled. *'Perhaps,'* she thought, *'things haven't gone as well for Mike as he claims.'*

She put a comforting hand over his hand and patted it, sympathetically.

"It's Mike's body," she said out loud, secretly hoping his decision not to have further hormone treatment would prove fatal. "If Mike doesn't want more treatment, he shouldn't have more treatment. Sometimes it's best just to leave it in God's hands."

"Mike isn't an oncologist," Mary said, seeing right through Valerie. "And neither is God."

"The Surgeon agreed with me," said Mike.

"He's not an oncologist either; all he wanted to do was cut your prostate out in the first place and leave you incontinent."

"Poor Mike," said Valerie, still patting his hand.

"Can we change the subject?" asked Rory, not from any sympathy for his brother but rather out of some vague fear that talking about prostate cancer might make it contagious.

"Cancer is sometimes hereditary," said Mary, as if reading Rory's thoughts.

She turned to Valerie.

"If it was Rory, wouldn't you want him to do everything possible to survive?"

"That depends," said Valerie.

She didn't expand on this answer but everybody had their own ideas about what it would depend on. And all of the ideas were pretty much the same.

If Mike were still alive, Valerie would do everything possible to keep Rory alive.

If Mike was dead and her father-in-law's estate was safely in Rory's hands, he could please himself.

Rory felt even more uncomfortable.

He yelled a second time, "I'm fed up with talking about bloody cancer."

It was a mistake.

They stopped talking about cancer but then they had to find something else to talk about and Mike raised a subject that had been intriguing him ever since he'd first arrived at the farm and taken a stroll down through the macadamia plantation to the rainforest and the creek below.

"What are those buildings down in the rainforest?" he asked.

There was a short, awkward silence as Valerie waited for Rory to reply.

When he didn't, she did.

"It's a Wellness Centre," she said.

"The Executors haven't mentioned a Wellness Centre to me," Mike frowned.

"Probably didn't want to bother you while you were ill," muttered Rory.

Mike shook his head.

"I've been getting all the Trust reports and accounts," he said. "There's been nothing."

"Because it's nothing to do with the Executors," said Valerie. "It's ours. Mine and Rory's. We paid for it."

"But it's on Trust Land," said Mike.

"So, what?" snapped Valerie? "It doesn't affect the Trust."

"It's Trust land," Mike repeated, his voice remaining calm but taking on an edge. "You can't build on somebody else's land."

Although Mary knew Mike was right, she really couldn't see the point of arguing about it.

"It doesn't matter, Mike" she said. "If you die before Rory it'll be theirs anyway. If he dies before you it'll be ours."

"The hell it will," said Valerie. "I paid for it. It's mine."

"How did you pay for it?" demanded Mike. "Did you get a mortgage? How did you get the bank to lend you money to build on somebody else's land?"

The silence told Mike everything he wanted to know. They'd told the bank they owned the land. Mike stopped short of voicing the accusation, but he wasn't happy.

Rather than directly reply to Mike, Rory muttered,

"We're talking to the Executor. We're telling him about the Wellness Centre."

"If you don't, I will," said Mike.

The dinner party went downhill from there.

CHAPTER FOUR

Mary couldn't sleep. She could feel and hear Mike tossing and turning and occasionally muttering under his breath.

She knew this would happen. Every time Mike and his brother got together it ended like this. Mary couldn't understand why she'd even agreed to come up to the farm, although she knew why Mike had been so keen to come. He had just wanted to stick it up Rory and Valerie. Show them how well he was. Tell them there was no chance they were getting their hands on his father's Trust.

But of course, as the Oncologist had said, they wouldn't know if the treatment had been a success for years, and in any case, for Mike to enjoy his victory, he had to have his emotions under control and that was never going to happen where his family was concerned.

Mike's family were his Achilles heel, his bête noir. Without them Mike was the most laidback person Mary knew; laidback almost to the point of laziness. It was this attitude that had first attracted her to him when they were both young trainee teachers. It contrasted nicely with her own, rather obsessive personality. Opposites attract, Mary told herself, and for the first twenty years of their marriage, theirs was an idyllic relationship; mainly because Mary had not met anybody from Mike's family.

He told her his mother had died when he was a teenager. He said he was estranged from his father. He never even mentioned a brother until he and Rory were called to their father's mansion where Bob Henry, their father's lawyer, advised them that their father was dying and that the two of them were to be the sole beneficiaries of his will.

They were gathered around the old man's bed, where Paddy lay in surprisingly good health and spirits for a man supposedly about to die. He was staring at Rory and Mike, judging their reactions. Rory was grinning; Mike remained quiet, waiting for the details.

Valerie couldn't hide her greed.

"The business isn't going to the oldest brother?" she asked. "That's the usual thing. They can't both run the business."

"I doubt if either of them can run the business," said Paddy, "But one of them will get the chance… eventually".

"Which one?" Rory demanded.

"Well…that's for you to decide," said the old man with a sly smile.

Knowing that he had now totally confused his two sons, Paddy refused to elucidate further. It was left to Bob Henry to explain.

"Your father's will is in the form of a tontine," he said.

Mike didn't react to the news but Mary looked shocked. Rory and Valeria just looked more confused.

"So, who gets the money?" Valerie asked.

"Whichever of them lives the longest," Mary told her.

"Smart girl you married," said Paddy to Mike.

"So, what happens to the money until then?" asked Rory, baffled.

"It will be held in trust," said Bob Henry, barely able to hide his pleasure since he was to be both trustee and executor of the will.

Mike just shook his head in disgust. Rory was more

vocal. He glared at his father.

"You bastard!" he said.

The old man laughed.

"Be careful, Rory," he said, "I'm not dead yet. I can always change my will."

Of course, he never would have changed his will. That would have meant the matter was resolved and that was precisely what Paddy didn't want. He wanted his two university-educated sons at each other's throats. He may have despised education but he wasn't stupid. He knew his sons despised him. To them he was the ignorant Irish Navvy who had driven their beloved mother to an early grave. Well, let's see how their University Educations helped them sort this mess out.

Seeing no point in discussing it, Mike got up, called to Mary to follow, and quietly walked out.

In the silence, driving home, Mary realised that she had been married to Mike for twenty years without ever really knowing him. She loved him. She knew he loved her. He had always seemed to be a bit reserved; as if he didn't care deeply about anything or anybody. Now she realised that he cared too much. He cared for his mother who was taken from him too early. He must have cared for his father, too. Like most kids he'd have tried hard to succeed; to make his father proud. What he hadn't understood, until it was too late, was that the more he excelled, the more his father resented him. How sad, Mary thought, her heart going out to the lonely little boy. Then her pity turned to a sort of dull anger. No doubt Rory had gone through the same process years earlier. He could have warned Mike, protected him, as a big brother should; but from what she had seen this afternoon, all he was interested in was looking out for himself. Now the tontine had made their alienation complete.

She never discussed any of this with Mike. She felt he'd probably be embarrassed by it, and she was right. Mike was obviously happier without his birth family intruding into the life he had made for himself. Mary, their son Matthew, his pretty wife, Charlotte, and little Lucas, their beloved grandson, were all the family Mike needed. As long as Mike was content, Mary was prepared to bury the subject; but she never forgot that day and her dislike of both Rory and Valerie, even after meeting them only once, remained as strong as ever.

It was another five years before Mike's father finally died and it was only then that Rory got in touch with Mike and Mary again and invited them up to the farm, as if it was already his. There he started trying to worm his way into Mike's good graces, trying to persuade him to contest the will. Mike wasn't interested. He didn't want his father's money. He didn't need it. He'd made his own way in life.

That was until he was told he had cancer. Overnight he realized that all his dreams of a comfortable future and retirement had been based on him and Mary working together for another ten years or so, in the jobs they both loved. Right now, they still had a mortgage. Their son, with his wife and child, lived in a rented apartment. They couldn't help them buy their own home. If Mike died, Mary would have nothing but her pension to live on and would probably retire still with a mortgage.

Mary tried to be practical. She told Mike they could downsize, maybe make a tree change; move to the country where property was, get rid of their mortgage. They could even lend young Matthew something towards a deposit if necessary.

"Oh," he said, "You've been thinking about it, have you? Thinking about how you'll all manage without me."

Mary knew Mike was being unreasonable. Mike knew Mike was being unreasonable.

So, the matter was never mentioned again and although Mary and Matthew were as supportive as they could be, Mike essentially went through the cancer treatment alone. Not wanting sympathy, afraid of affection; just as he'd been after his mother died and before he met Mary.

When the treatment was over, Mike felt a huge weight come off him. The Oncologist might say they wouldn't know for years if the treatment was successful but that implied that he would be around for years to find out. Death didn't seem so fearful if he still had time to do the things he wanted to do; set his affairs in order. Not that he knew exactly what he wanted to do. But the one thing he did know was that he wanted to stick it up his brother, Rory.

Hence his acceptance of the invitation to the farm.

Mike had intended to enjoy it. He'd told Mary to pack for a week at least. They hadn't even been at the farm a full day, let alone a week, and Mike was already tossing and turning, not sleeping, convinced that Rory and Valerie had built the Wellness Centre because they fully expected to own the whole farm soon; fully expected that he would be dead, and had planned accordingly.

Mary didn't know what to say or do.

"Let it go," she said eventually. "In the end it won't affect us."

"They're bloody thieves," Mike muttered.

"Not thieves, surely," said Mary, trying to be reasonable.

"They're building on land that doesn't belong to them,"

Mike insisted.

"That doesn't make them thieves. At worst it makes them squatters."

The idea appealed to Mary.

"You should tell Valerie that," she giggled, "I don't think Valerie sees herself as a squatter."

"It's not funny," snapped Mike as he clambered out of bed and went groping around for his lap top.

"What are you doing?" Mary demanded.

"Writing to Bob Henry, the executor," Mike said.

"At three o'clock in the morning?" Mary couldn't believe it. "Can't you leave it 'til tomorrow?"

"We won't be here tomorrow," said Mike, "As soon as I've sent off this email, we'll pack up and go home."

"No way," said Mary, "you promised me a week's holiday. After what you've been through, what we've both been through, we need it. If you want to leave, fine. We'll head north. The Queensland border is only an hour away. We'll go there for our holiday."

Rory and Valerie must have heard them leaving. There was a lot of door slamming and swearing. The wild brute of a dog they kept at the farm barked its head off. And even when Mike went up to the dog's pen, kicked the fence and screamed at the dog, there was no sign of Rory or Valerie.

"Thank God for small mercies," thought Mary, as Mike, with much revving of the engine, reversed out of their parking space and drove out through the farm gate, back to the highway and turned north, towards Queensland.

With the freeway running all the way to the Queensland border, on past the Gold Coast, and then circumventing Brisbane on the Airport Bypass, by dawn Mike had driven as far as the Sunshine Coast before Mary could persuade him to stop for breakfast.

After eating, Mike begrudgingly let Mary drive and he dozed off for a while, only to wake as Mary drove into Hervey Bay.

"Hervey Bay," he groaned, "God's waiting room."

It was the name Sydneysiders gave to Hervey Bay because so many people retired there. With nothing to do, they mostly drank themselves to death.

"We don't have to stay here," Mary said, "Let's head to Townsville. We can go out to Magnetic Island, inland to Charters Towers and the Dinosaur Trail at Winton."

"It's a long drive," Mike protested.

"We've got time," said Mary.

And, since she had the steering wheel, Mary continued to drive north while Mike sulked for a while, then dozed off to sleep again.

CHAPTER FIVE

Mary drove for the next hour with Mike snoring fitfully in the seat beside her.

Then suddenly he sat bolt upright, a big smile on his face.

"You're right, you know," he said, "It doesn't affect us if Rory and Valerie build a Wellness Centre on the farm. In fact, if we do end up owning the farm, it'll only make the property more valuable."

"That's what I said," said Mary.

Mike didn't reply; he just looked happily out of the window.

"So, you're not going to do anything about it?" asked Mary. "Not tell the bank?"

Mike shrugged.

"It's not worth it, is it?" he said, "Life's too short."

Mary had guessed all along that Mike would do nothing about it. Not because he thought what Rory and Valerie were doing was right, but because he was just too lazy to carry it through. He'd always been like that. Even more so now, after the cancer treatment.

Mike went back to sleep, and Mary decided to let the matter drop, sit back and enjoy the ride and what remained of their holiday.

The next few days were some of the happiest Mary and Mike had spent together since Matthew left home. Mike never mentioned the Wellness Centre or the will except when Bob Henry replied to his email to say that the Trust were talking to Rory and would grant him a ten-year lease on the land on which the Wellness Centre stood.

"Will that satisfy the bank?" Mary asked.

"Doubt if they've told the bank," Mike shrugged, as if it didn't matter. "Bob Henry was dad's lawyer for years. He must be a crook. How else would dad have gotten away with all those dodgy houses he built? Every time something went wrong, they'd just wind up the company and start a new one."

Mary was surprised that Mike was taking it all so well, but she didn't push the subject, not while Mike seemed so happy.

North of Townsville they found a little place near the water on Airbnb, and between trips to Magnetic Island and inland to Charters Towers, they spent their time eating in little restaurants and cafes and peering at the ads in local real estate office windows. Not that they were looking for a place to buy, but like many tourists before them they liked to compare prices and dream of what could be but probably never would be. Unemployment in North Queensland was about twice the national average and this was reflected in the property prices.

"You know," Mike said, remembering the conversation they'd had more than a year ago and which had caused such an argument, "You were right. We could make a Tree Change. Downsize. Even after paying off the mortgage in Sydney we'd have enough money to buy a house up here, a little tinnie, a campervan."

Mary remembered the conversation, too. She wasn't exactly happy to be reminded of it.

"You've changed your tune,' she said, "You said I was planning for your death."

"Yeah, well," said Mike, "I was ill, wasn't I? Scared I suppose. It's different now. We could do this together. We could even retire."

"I don't want to retire," said Mary.

"It wouldn't be compulsory. I'm sure they need teachers up here. They need them everywhere outside of the big cities. You could still work. I could write a book."

"About what?"

Mike shrugged.

"My bloody family for a start," he said.

"Nobody would ever believe it," said Mary.

"No," Mike agreed, but the thought didn't bother him too much because, as Mary knew, Mike would never write a book even if they did move north. He'd probably just get bored stupid, mope around and wish they'd stayed in Sydney.

Mary didn't tell him this. And she was too smart to want to continue the animosity that the talk of a Tree Change had cause earlier. Instead, she acted as if she were taking Mike's plans seriously.

"I couldn't leave my little ones in the middle of the school year," she said, "It would upset them too much."

Mary was a primary school teacher and, if they did move north, she certainly wouldn't want to disrupt the lives of her little first graders by having them change teachers in the middle of the year.

"You wouldn't need to," said Mike, "It'll take us to the end of the school year at least to sell our house in Sydney. Then you could come up here, start afresh in a new school with a new class of ankle-biters."

Mary didn't like Mike referring to her children as ankle biters, but she resisted the temptation to snap at him. Instead she just put more obstacles in his way.

"What about little Lucas?" she asked, referring to their grandson who was the apple of Mike's eye. "You'd miss him."

"He'd love visiting us. Go boating, fishing. We'll probably see more of him up here than we do now in Sydney," said Mike.

"And what about your health?"

"That's the beauty of the idea," said Mike. "More people retire to Queensland that anywhere else in Australia. With whole communities like Hervey Bay and Tewantin designed just to care for the aged, up here people don't die. They live forever."

Mary didn't raise any more objections. She knew putting too many obstacles in his way would only make him obstinate. He might go ahead with a move north just to prove Mary couldn't tell him what to do.

"Well," she said, "If we're going to move up here permanently, we'd better take a good look around while we're here; see what the area has to offer."

"Yeah," said Mike, his enthusiasm already waning at the prospect of making some kind of effort. "Course, we'll have to be back in Sydney for the start of next term, so there's a limit on what we can see."

And Mary knew Mike wasn't really serious about making a Tree Change. He was just daydreaming.

Despite this, and mainly pushed on by Mary, they filled their days seeing places and trying things they'd never done before. Fishing, snorkelling. Mike said they could even learn to scuba dive if they moved north permanently; go camping in the rainforest, up the Cassowary Coast, or in the Outback. That made Mary laugh: in nearly thirty years of marriage, she had never even managed to get him into a tent.

"You won't get me in one now," he told her, "We'll get a little campervan with a boat on the top, an awning on the side where we can sit and watch the sunset. You can paint. We can go anywhere. Complete freedom."

Mary was pretty sure the reality wouldn't be quite like that. She'd be tied to her job during term-time and Lucas's visits during the school holidays would prevent too much travelling. But it didn't worry her. She was sure that after a few weeks back in Sydney Mike would forget about the whole thing. She'd just let things run their course.

And she still didn't worry when Mike suggested that they call in on Rory and Valerie on the way home and tell them the good news. In fact, she suspected that this was the main motive behind the whole dream; to let Rory know that Mike intended to be around for a long time and that the next chapter in his life was just starting, not finishing.

As they drove up to the farmhouse it seemed strangely silent. Even the mutt in his pen was quiet: probably traumatised by his last encounter with Mike, thought Mary.

The only person in the house was Margaret, the cleaner who came in three days a week to clean a house that never got dirty because nobody was ever there.

"Where's Rory and Val?" Mike asked, cheerily

"Mrs. Maguire is in Thailand hiring staff for the Wellness Centre" said Margaret.

Obviously, Margaret wasn't on first name terms with her employers.

"And where's Rory?"

"He's on the Gold Coast," said Margaret. "Mr. McGuire always goes to the Gold Coast while Mrs. McGuire's away in Thailand. I don't know what he does there."

Although her tone suggested that she had a pretty good idea.

Mike pretended not to notice

"So, they're still going ahead with the Wellness Centre?" he said, "Even though they'll have to pay rent?"

"Rent?" queried Margaret.

"On the Wellness Centre," Mike carried on, despite Mary's warning look. "They have to rent the land it's standing on. It belongs to the farm."

"I thought Mr. and Mrs. McGuire owned the farm?" Margaret said, confused.

"Ah, well," Mike nodded, "I suppose up here, everybody does. Still never mind. Just tell them we called in. Tell them we're moving north to Queensland. Tell them I'm in rude health. I expect to live forever. I'm sure they'll be pleased."

"And you are?" asked Margaret.

"Rory's brother," said Mike, "Owner of the farm, once my dad's will is settled."

As they drove away Mary couldn't help scolding Mike for telling Margaret that Rory didn't own the farm.

"I always tell my Grade Ones not to tell tales," she said, "You should have learnt by now."

"I bet you also tell them not to tell lies," said Mike.

"That's not the point," said Mary, "You shouldn't tell tales. You know what gossips these country women are."

"Sorry," said Mike.

But he wasn't.

Nor was Margaret the Cleaning Lady. She would have plenty to tell the girls at the Bowling Club that weekend: they didn't even own the farm, but Valerie was off to Thailand alone, again, and Rory was chasing his tart up on the Gold Coast.

CHAPTER SIX

Margaret wasn't quite correct. Rory wasn't on the Gold Coast chasing his tart. In fact, he was doing quite the opposite. He was there trying to get rid of her. She'd become too expensive. Everything had become too expensive.

Val's bloody Wellness Centre was costing a fortune and it wasn't even open yet. And having to pay rent on it was the last straw. Rory had only agreed to the rental agreement because he had no choice, but he wasn't going to sign the rental agreement. That would put in writing, evidence that he didn't own the farm. If the Bank got hold of that, he'd be finished.

He couldn't avoid paying the rent, of course. The Executor would just take the money out of his share of the Trust's profits. But if it ever came to light that he didn't own the land, he would simply claim he never said he did; the Bank must have misunderstood.

Anyway, by then, hopefully, the Wellness Centre would be making a fortune. If it wasn't, Rory was doomed. Unless bloody Mike carked it, but that seemed unlikely given that his cancer treatment had ended, and successfully too, apparently.

The real problem was that Rory had no idea whether the Wellness Centre would work or not. It was entirely Valerie's idea. For years now Rory and Valerie had been living virtually separate lives. They had no kids. No grandkids. Bored stupid with just each other for company on the farm after Rory had had to flee the City in disgrace, they'd started taking separate holidays: Valerie to a ridiculously expensive retreat in Thailand while Rory joined a golf club on the Gold Coast and spent his time there with his equally expensive mistress.

In fact, the only bit of good luck Rory had was when Valerie slipped and broke her collarbone in the Thai retreat's pool. Terrified that Valerie would sue them, the resort had paid her medical bills and given her a Life-Membership which meant she could spend two weeks a year there completely free. Not including the business class airfares there and back, of course.

It was when she read the valuation that the Thai retreat had put on the lifetime membership that Valerie got the idea of starting her own Wellness Centre. She started collecting the Thai retreat's brochures, questioning the staff, learning the ropes and even stealing the client list; until she was confident that she could set up her own Wellness Centre down in the rainforest, even if it meant cutting down a few old-growth rainforest trees in the process.

Valerie decided to play it smart. She wouldn't try to compete with the week-long sojourns in Thailand; rather she would concentrate on weekend breaks. Short breaks for the tired and jaded executives from Sydney, Melbourne and Brisbane. Flying up to Thailand for just a weekend would be unthinkable. But a forty-minute flight to Lismore and a fifteen-minute drive to the farm, and every executive in the Eastern States would be less than an hour away from peace and tranquillity.

The Wellness Centre was almost an exact copy of the Thai retreat. The same timber roofs, timber floors and walls. The same essence burning from the same joss sticks. But Valerie's Wellness Centre needed something more to convince the jaded city executives to part with their hard-earned cash. They needed reassurance that the treatment they got in Northern New South Wales would be as good as the treatment they got in Thailand.

That was where Valerie had her brainwave. She would steal the staff from the Thai retreat. Not only steal them but boast about it in her sales brochures and publicity. But importing workers was an expensive process and the Wellness Centre wasn't even open yet so it wasn't making any money. Rory had to rein in expenses; and his biggest expense was Roxette.

Roxette Simpson was a girl born after her time. In fact, she was a girl almost not born at all. Her mother named her Roxette after the singer who had the hit, "It must have been love" in the late eighties.

"It must have been love, but it's over now."
It was a constant reminder that her father had shot through long before Roxette was born and that if Roxette's grandparents hadn't been devout Catholics, Roxette would have been an abortion rather than a burden on her mother.

Not that this lack of maternal affection bothered Roxette. She barely lived in the real world. She was a dreamer who had her future all mapped out from an early age. She would be a Gold Coast Meter Maid where, in her gold lame bikini, she would attract the attention of a film producer or casting director from the nearby Warner Brothers' Studios and be launched to stardom via the Casting Couch.

Unfortunately for Roxette, by the time her figure had filled out enough to do justice to her gold lame bikini, parking meters on the Gold Coast no longer took coins but credit cards. Meter Maids no longer put sixpences into meters to save motorists from a fine; instead, they acted as an advisory body, telling visitors to the Gold Coast how to operate the card-taking meters and where the best attractions were. This was hardly likely to attract the attention of a Warner Brothers' Studios producer. Besides, the *'Me Too'* movement was beginning to rear its head, making the casting couch a far less reliable pathway to fame. She did however attract the attention of Rory, driving into the Gold Coast and looking for a parking space for his Range Rover. A brief instruction on how to use the parking meter led to a dinner invitation, and although Rory wasn't a film producer, Roxette knew she had hit the jackpot.

Roxette would have resented the term, *'Kept Woman'* and certainly didn't feel in any way that she was Rory's property. She lived her own life. He had an apartment that he only used when he was on the Gold Coast, playing golf while Valerie was away in her Thai Chakra Healing Retreat. What harm could it do if Roxette lived in the apartment when Rory wasn't there; and also, when he was? Living rent-free meant Roxette didn't have to work and she had time, and Rory's money, to spend on gym classes, dancing classes and acting classes, for she still dreamt of stardom and looked out for any random film producers or casting directors who happened to frequent the Gold Coast nightspots.

But time was running out and she knew her chances of fame were slipping away.

Like most Meter Maids, you could hardly call Roxette, *'New Age'* but again like most Meter Maids, she had a passing interest in alternate medicines, diets, yoga and crystals. Enough anyway to query why it was that Rory's wife went to a Chakra Healing Retreat in Thailand when

Chakra was Hindu; from India?

Rory had never thought to ask; but he did ask, after Roxette asked him.

"Most of India smells," had been Valerie's reply, "Besides their ashrams are so basic. They don't even have swimming pools. You have to bathe in the river. And God knows how many kidneys that river has been through before the water reaches you."

"Don't even serve a decent, dry martini," Rory had muttered facetiously, bringing a stinging retort from Valerie, despite the fact that she knew very well that the wine waiter at the Thai retreat did, in fact, make a very passable dry martini for just a few thousand baht, when the Yogi wasn't looking. Served in a chilled water glass, the martinis had the added attraction of being not only good but forbidden. Valerie had already decided they would be an integral part of her own Retreat in the Rainforest.

Rory's problem was that, although he was a charlatan, happy to cheat his stockbroking clients and lie to the bank to get a loan, he was also a coward. The thought of telling Roxette that he was throwing her out of his apartment and cancelling her acting and dance classes, not to mention her gym subscription, filled him with terror.

On the drive from the Northern New South Wales hinterland to the Gold Coast, he kept practicing what he would say. He considered borrowing his brother's prostate cancer as an excuse for why he couldn't keep up the apartment and pay for her classes, but he thought she wouldn't want to sleep with him if he had prostate cancer.

Then he considered manufacturing an argument with her, after they'd slept together of course, then storming out and cancelling the lease on the apartment without telling her. But he wasn't very good at manufacturing anger. Besides, Roxette wasn't the sort of girl to take things lying down. She'd probably turn up at the farm and confront him when Valerie was there.

In the end, like Valerie, Rory also had a brainwave: He decided to tell the truth. He and Valerie were building a Retreat. It would cost a lot of money but it would make a lot of money. So initially, Rory would have to cancel the lease on the apartment but in a matter of months, even weeks, he would be back, richer than ever, looking to buy an apartment, a boat, who knows what?

Roxette sat very still while Rory gave her the news. A strange little frown appeared on her brow. Then it cleared and she smiled.

"That's fantastic," she said. "I can be a teacher at the Retreat."

"You don't know anything about Yoga or Chakra," Rory said, taken aback

"Neither do you," countered Roxette, "And you're opening the Retreat."

"Besides I can take a course," she went on. "Take Yoga lessons. My friend took an intensive ten-week course, now she's a qualified Yoga Teacher, Healer and Guide. She's a shaman."

"Sounds like a con job to me," said Rory,

Roxette looked at him and smiled as if he were a silly little boy.

"Rory," she said, gently, "This Retreat you're building… you're telling me that isn't a con job?"

As he drove back to the Northern New South Wales Hinterland, Rory couldn't understand how his mission to get rid of Roxette had ended up costing him more money. They had agreed, at least Roxette had agreed that they would keep the apartment on until the Wellness Centre or Retreat or whatever was up and running, then Roxette would move south and move in.

In the meantime, she would enrol in a course to be a Yogi and Spiritual Healer, which cost $4,000 and which Rory would pay for. As Roxette pointed out, she would have to cancel her classes in dance, and in acting, and her gym membership, so it wouldn't cost much more.

Rory had suggested that since she would be moving south to Northern New Wales sooner or later anyway, she should move now and save on the rental on the Gold Coast apartment, but Roxette was having none of that.

"I can't turn up in Northern New South Wales as an actress one week, then a few weeks later be accepted as a shaman," she said. "I have to turn up as the completed article. Fully qualified."

"In ten weeks?" Rory had asked, sarcastically, but Roxette lacked Valerie understanding of Rory's sarcasm so she didn't snap back at him.

Instead she looked thoughtful for a moment.

"I'll have to change my name when I'm a shaman," she said. "Roxette doesn't sound new age; more eighties rock. My friend says the latest trend is combining ancient Hindu Chakra Healing with the even older wisdom of our ancient indigenous peoples, so I should choose something Australian, but mystical."

"*Daintree*," she decided suddenly. "I'll call myself Daintree; after the Rainforest."

CHAPTER SEVEN

Valerie had been more successful than Rory on her mission to Thailand. For little more than the Australian basic wage she had managed to snare not one but two employees from the Thai Retreat: a yoga instructor and a masseuse.

"Don't think that means you're going to get free massages," she told Rory.

Rory didn't mind. He'd made his own arrangements for free massages. So, when Valerie gave him the resumes of the two Thai girls to put in the Retreat's sales brochure, he added his own, highly embellished resume of the famous Queensland yoga teacher and healer, raised in the oldest rainforest in the world, *'Daintree'* Simpson.

Valerie looked at the addition with some suspicion.

"Who is this Daintree Simpson? she asked.

"A new wave shaman," Rory replied, blithely, "She combines the ancient Hindu Chakra wisdom with the even older Australian Indigenous wisdom. It's the latest thing apparently."

"Never heard of her," Valerie said.

"Have you heard of any Australian shaman?" Rory asked, "Anybody you don't have to spend a fortune to go and visit?"

Valerie ignored the question.

"I hope she's not expensive," she said.

"She'll be paid on commission," said Rory, knowing that if Valerie thought *'Daintree'* was costing her nothing, she wouldn't bother about her.

"If we're going to combine Hindu and Indigenous mysticism, perhaps we should give the Retreat an indigenous name?" Valerie suggested. "There are Davidson Plum trees in our rainforest, aren't there? Perhaps we could use the indigenous word for Davidson Plum?"

But when she looked up the name and discovered it was '*Ooray*', she wasn't quite so sure.

"It sounds Australian, but it doesn't sound mystical," she said, "I think we'll stick to our original idea of The Golden Topaz Rainforest Retreat."

Rory had no idea what the significance of the Golden Topaz was, nor did he care. So, he agreed, and all that remained for him to do was send the sales brochure off to the printers, buy himself a pair of sandals, a pair of chinos and a cheesecloth shirt, and head off to join '*Daintree*' on her very short journey to enlightenment.

Mike and Mary's journey north took a lot longer.

As Mary had predicted, Mike returned home full of enthusiasm. He told Matthew and his grandson, Lucas that they were moving north. He spoke to a mate at the golf club, a real estate agent named Damian Koh, and asked him to come around and value the house.

Damian was on the doorstep the following morning, keen to look through the house, which he soon found out was a reflection of Mike's character. That is, very comfortable but with a lot of little maintenance jobs that needed doing; jobs that would greatly increase the value of the house, in Damian's opinion. Mike wasn't sure that it was worth the effort, or the money, to do expensive renovation work. He told Mary,

"A buyer would want to renovate the house himself. Spending money on it now would just be a waste."

Knowing the best way to dissuade Mike from doing

anything was to pretend to be supportive, Mary suggested that Mike get a second opinion; call in another agent.

"I can't do that," said Mike. "Damian'll think I'm going behind his back."

So, Mike did nothing and he and Mary slipped back into their old routine. Mary went back to work. Mike went back to work. In fact, he returned to work with a new enthusiasm. He even agreed to write, direct and produce the annual school play. Mary didn't point out to him that this meant that he was committed to staying in Sydney until Christmas. She thought there was no need. She was pretty sure Mike's plans had been put on hold indefinitely.

And she would have been right if Rory and Valerie hadn't run out of money, meaning that they couldn't put the final touches to their Rainforest Retrat: the swimming pool, the spa, and the sauna. Nor could they afford a liquor license. None of these were things you'd expect to find in a true Chakra retreat, but then Rory and Valerie weren't looking to attract people on the road to enlightenment. There was too much competition for that market in nearby Mullumbimby and Byron Bay.

They were looking at the Jaded Executive market. People who just wanted to pamper themselves but also kid themselves and others that what they were doing was good for them and making them better executives. How else could they get their companies to pay for these junkets?

Valerie had already called in the architects, insisting not only on the swimming pool, the spa, and the sauna, but also a plunge pool in the rainforest, with crystal clear water running from the natural spring. It would be the focal point of the Retreat, she said; the connection with the rainforest. Although privately she doubted any of the executives would be foolhardy enough to get into the pool, especially in winter. They'd prefer the heated spa and the even warmer sauna.

Now Rory was saying they couldn't afford any of these things and he couldn't get any more money out of the bank. As usual, it was Valerie who had to come up with the solution.

She consulted a lawyer friend in Sydney; far enough away from Northern New South Wales for the enquiry not to become public knowledge. She was looking for money and she was looking for a way to get hold of the title to the land on which the Retreat stood, but she also wanted title to the farmhouse and she wanted guaranteed access through the farm to the Retreat and the house. What she didn't want, what she couldn't afford, was to buy the entire macadamia farm.

Her lawyer friend discovered that the Trust held a Company Title over the farm. It was possible to buy shares in the Company and in return receive exclusive possession of specific areas of the property, as well as access to the roads, rainforest and farm. All Valerie and Rory had to do was convince the trustee to sell them shares in the company. There was only one problem. They had no money. Not only that, they had taken out a considerable mortgage with the bank to complete construction. Who was going to pay for all this?

To Valerie the answer seemed obvious. If her father-in-law's Trust owned the farm, then it should pay for the improvements the Retreat would bring to the property as a whole. Rory thought there was no way the executors would pay to give somebody else title over the Trust's own property but Valerie had a secret weapon; at least she thought she did. She was sure the Chief Executor, Bob Henry, had always fancied her.

Bob Henry was a singularly unattractive man, but in an emergency, needs must, so she sent Rory off to play golf on the Gold Coast when Bob next visited the farm to inspect the trees and discuss business with the farm manager.

Normally Rory would have been there to greet him. Normally Rory would have objected to Valerie dealing with Bob on her own. But he and Daintree had become much closer as she completed the course on Chakra Healing, and Rory was quite keen to get back to the Gold Coast to learn more about tantric sex.

The flaw in Valerie's plan was that Bob didn't fancy her at all.

The way he looked at her, which Valerie had taken as a sexual interest, was in fact a look of mild curiosity. He couldn't understand why Rory had divorced his first, very pleasant wife, for the older and less attractive Valerie. To use a car dealer's analogy, as Bob often did, he couldn't understand why Rory had traded in his as-new wife for, not a second-hand, but a third-hand old banger, since Valerie had been married twice before.

So, when Bob arrived at the farm to find Rory wasn't there, only Valerie in a very skimpy dress, offering him a drink at eleven o'clock in the morning, he was not pleased. To make matters worse Bob was xenophobic, so the offer of a massage from the petite but rather muscular Thai masseuse, didn't appeal either.

He demanded to know where Rory was.

Valerie said he couldn't be contacted. He was playing golf at his Gold Coast Club.

Bob had flown in to Coolangatta airport on the Gold

Coast that morning and had hired a car to drive to the farm. The drive had taken him less than an hour down the freeway so he knew Rory could be back at the farm in an hour. He insisted that Valerie call him immediately.

"Of course," she said, barely keeping the smile on her face. "Just in time for lunch. We have an excellent chef at the Retreat"

An hour later, Rory arrived, and he was not alone.

Daintree had decided, given that things obviously hadn't gone well with Valerie and Bob, that she should step in.

Valerie had never met Roxette. Even if she had, it isn't certain that she would have recognized her as Daintree. Gone was the platinum blonde, carefully quaffed hair. Daintree had allowed it to grow out and the golden brown locks now hung down over her shoulders, flowing loose. A crystal on a chain decorated her forehead. The gold lame bikini had been replaced by a light, diaphanous cheesecloth dress and it was obvious to anyone with half an eye that Daintree wasn't wearing any underwear.

Bob had two eyes. Valerie wasn't impressed, but Bob certainly was; from the moment Daintree first looked at him, and gave a little gasp.

"What?" he asked her, concerned.

"Your aura," she said, "It's broken. Blocked at the Sacral Chakra."

Bob was pretty certain she was taking the mickey.

"Aura?" he said, "Nobody's ever complained about my aura before."

"Probably because they can't see it," said Daintree, ignoring his sarcasm, "Only the most sensitive and experienced healers can detect it."

And, in case Bob didn't buy this, Daintree added a little-known scientific fact that she'd found on the Internet.

"The Aura has been measured by NASA scientists using Kirlian photography," she said, "The body has an electro-magnetic field, just like Gaia, the earth, and all other living things."

Bob had heard of the earth's electro- magnetic field. He had even heard of NASA. So, he decided to play along.

"And my aura is broken, is it?" he asked, barely keeping the smirk from his face.

"Broken, blocked, call it what you will," said Daintree, "There is a blockage surrounding your second Sacral Chakra. The Chakra associated with pleasure, sexuality, nurture, and change."

She spaced the words, letting them breathe and giving them extra gravitas.

"Do you feel the need for change?" she asked.

The truth was Bob was very much in need of change. Despite his rude manner and crude language on occasions, he was probably the most sexually hung-up lawyer ever to sit for his final exams. Like Rory and Mike, Bob's problems started with his father who, when at twenty-seven, Bob had never even brought a girl home to meet his parents, enquired in a loud voice at the Christmas family gathering whether Bob was a poofter?

Bob wasn't a poofter. He was just painfully awkward and unsuccessful with women.

Eventually he summoned up the courage to marry a mousey little secretary from his legal practice. Not through any great passion but primarily to stop his father embarrassing him.

The marriage had proved a mild success. His wife was supportive and even more awkward than he was. Sex never got past the missionary position and in the last ten years hadn't even achieved that. A fact that Daintree recognized the moment she saw him. Although, whether she knew this because she had really become a Healer or whether she knew it because of her vast experience of men when she was a Meter Maid, not even Daintree herself could have told you.

In any event she moved closer to Bob and said,

"There are things that can be done that can repair your aura."

Bob felt himself blushing.

"I don't think I'll bother," he muttered,

"Oh, it's no bother," said Daintree. "It's what I'm here for"

Bob was torn between his fascination with Daintree and his need to get out of a situation he couldn't control. In the end he insisted that Rory take him on a tour of inspection around the farm in Rory's Range Rover, and the two set off, leaving Daintree and Valerie alone.

"I suppose I'd better tell Chef there are two more for lunch," Valerie said.

And she disappeared in the direction of the rainforest and the Retreat kitchen, with her nose in the air.

The tour of the farm didn't take long. Partially because Rory didn't really know much about the place, leaving as he did the running of the farm to Darren, their one and only farmhand; and partially because he delighted in driving up the steepest hills on the farm, causing Bob to fear that any moment the vehicle would tip over and he would die.

Nevertheless, by the time they got back to the Retreat, Daintree had already had time to explore the place and had taken a golden topaz crystal and a book on Chakra Healing from the Retreat's shop, which she presented to

Bob on his return.

"What's this?" he asked suspiciously.

"Just a book and a crystal I sense is right for you," said Daintree. "Just put it in your bag. Something to read on the flight home."

Daintree didn't attempt to talk about Bob's aura or any new-age philosophy during lunch, but she did sit so close to him that her ample bosom, no longer restrained by a bra, almost flopped into his water glass. In fact, on one occasion Daintree had to move his glass aside in order to avoid an accident.

Eventually Rory suggested that Valerie should accompany him to the kitchen to prepare dessert. Everybody knew he had done this to give Daintree and Bob time alone together. Even so Daintree didn't speak. Didn't mention Bob's aura. She just waited for Bob to start the conversation.

"Do Rory and Valerie have auras?" he asked eventually.

"Oh yes," said Daintree.

"And are they broken?"

"Blocked," said Daintree, "But not in the way your aura is blocked. Although they are blocked in the same area, The Sacral, second Chakra, the Svadhistana."

Bob had no idea what she was talking about.

"They have sexual problems, do they?" he asked, hopefully.

"In a way," said Daintree, "They have entitlement problems. There are two types of Sacral Personality. The martyr, who feels that he, or she, deserves their sexual and emotional misfortune. And the Sovereigns who think the whole world owes them a living. Rory and Valerie are Sovereigns. That's why they can build this Retreat on somebody else's land. They feel they're entitled."

This rang true to Bob, and even his unimaginative mind could put two and two together. If Rory and Valerie were the Sovereigns, then he was the Martyr.

"Not necessarily you," Daintree counselled, "It could be your wife. She may be sexually repressed. Unable to discuss her sexual desires and fantasies with you."

"Sexual desires and fantasies?" queried Bob, "I don't think she has any of those."

Daintree put a comforting hand on Bob's hand and he felt a distinct stirring behind his sacral chakra that he hadn't felt in years.

"Poor Bob," she said. "Everybody has desires and fantasies. I wish I could help. I wish we could get your wife up to the Retreat but I guess that's impossible now."

"Why?" asked Bob.

"Well, I was going to be here," said Daintree, "But Rory says they can't afford me. They can't afford anything, so they'll just rely on their Thai employees and Valerie."

"Not that I think Valerie has any claim to being a healer," she added. "The place will probably fail. Fall into disrepair. Pity. It's a magical spot with special vibrations."

When Rory and Valerie returned, laden with bounty from the farm, macadamia nuts, Davidson Plums from the rainforest, and a load of other stuff that Valerie had just picked up at the market in Byron Bay, Bob didn't waste time beating about the bush.

"Why aren't you employing Daintree at the Retreat?" he demanded to know.

Valerie looked at Daintree suspiciously, but Rory was a lot quicker on the uptake.

"It's unfortunate, but we just can't afford her."

"Nonsense," said Bob. "You can't afford not to have her. Without her, you've got nothing. Neither of you have any gift for healing, or even any empathy for that matter. How could you possibly make enough money to pay for shares in the Company Title? If you want the Trust to invest, Daintree will have to run the place."

"It's not her Retreat," Valerie spluttered out. "It's mine."

"Of course, it is," Rory assured her. "Bob doesn't mean Daintree would run the business, but she'd run the Retreats, the courses in yoga and chakra healing."

Daintree feigned surprise that Rory would suggest such a thing but Bob was ahead of him.

"Too right," he said, "I might even send the wife up for a visit."

After the meal, Bob said Rory should show him the business plan for the Retreat.

"Can't lose sight of the realities," he said, "The figures have to add up"

"Absolutely," said Rory, and he drove Bob back up to the house where the business plan was kept in the office.

Valerie smiled and waved them goodbye, but as soon as they were out of sight, she turned on Daintree and glared at her.

"Don't think you're taking over the Retreat," she said, "I can't believe he fell for all your New Age bollocks."

"I doubt he did," said Daintree, smiling sweetly, "I think it was more the powdered Viagra I put into his water glass."

CHAPTER EIGHT

Whilst Rory and Valerie's future plans seemed to be back on track, Mike's plans hit a speed bump. The Oncologist, his GP, and Mary, had all insisted that he take regular blood tests to see if his cancer treatment had been successful. And, as he always did, Mike insisted on getting a copy of the pathology report direct from the lab. He noted that while his testosterone reading still remained low, his PSA, his Prostate Specific Antigens reading had risen from zero - where it had languished during the time he was having the hormone injections - up to 1.6. He had no idea whether this was good or bad, but he felt certain that the Oncologist would see it as an opportunity to get him back on to hormone therapy.

His fears were amplified as he sat in the Oncologist's waiting room. A couple had come out after a consultation; the inevitable small, brow-beaten man and the large woman, large in both stature and voice.

"Isn't that wonderful?" the woman enquired of her husband, "We've been coming here for ten years, and your cancer still hasn't returned."

Mike groaned inwardly. He couldn't face another ten years of consultations, even if the alternative was death.

He entered the consultation room in a fit of depression and it only got worse as the consultation went exactly as he'd expected.

The Oncologist said his PSA was rising. Mike pointed out that it was still very low, so was his testosterone reading. The Oncologist barely acknowledged that he had spoken.

"If your PSA keeps rising, we'll have to put you back on hormone treatment,' he said. "We can't let it progress beyond three. I'll arrange another blood test for you next month, then we'll see how we're progressing."

While the Oncologist typed the instructions for a further blood test onto the pro-forma on his computer, Mike asked him,

"These hormones. As I understand it, they can't cure the cancer."

"No," agreed the Oncologist, "But they'll slow the symptoms. You'll feel better for a lot longer."

"And I'll live longer? Mike asked.

"Well, no," said the Oncologist. "Your symptoms will be delayed but when they come, they'll progress far more quickly. Data shows you'll live about the same amount of time. But you'll have a much better quality of life."

Mike wasn't sure that he agreed with that prognosis. Since he'd stopped the hormone treatment, his energy levels had risen again. He was a little tired after a day's teaching, especially if it included auditions for the school play, but at least he got through the day. When he was having hormone treatment, he had felt so listless that he'd had to take time off from school and spent his days mostly snoozing and waking in a confused haze.

'Was that a better quality of life?' he wondered.

It took strength of will for Mike to forget about his PSA and concentrate on school, the school play and his family, but the PSA test hung over him like the Sword of Damocles. Inevitably he would wake in the middle of the night and stare at the ceiling for hours, his mind in a vortex of conflicting thoughts.

Even so, he didn't take the test after a month, or even after five weeks. But after six weeks Mary insisted on him going to the pathologist, even waking him long before he needed to go to school and giving him a packed breakfast to eat in the Common Room after he'd had the test.

The test came back. The reading was 2.4.

Mike was no Maths teacher but he had a basic understanding of parabolas and graphs. His PSA had risen from zero to 1.6 in the three months after the end of his treatment; 2.4 in the following six weeks. The curve was rising and the rise, while not getting steeper, was constant.

He suggested to the Oncologist that since it was nearly five months since his treatment ended and since his PSA was still at an acceptably low level, they should have another blood test in six months' time and see how they go.

The Oncologist thought they should test him again after another month.

Even though Mike felt perfectly well, better than he'd felt for years, he was sure that the next blood test would take his PSA above the dreaded 3 level and they'd be injecting a huge hormone pellet the size of a .22 rifle bullet into the muscle near his umbilical cord, where it would slowly dissolve for six months and stop the production of testosterone for at least a year, not to mention destroying ten percent of what was left of his skeletal mass.

The prospect seemed even more dire, coming as it did just when Bob Henry sent him a pamphlet with the announcement of the opening of the Golden Topaz Rainforest Retreat.

The circumstances made Mike irrationally angry. He knew now that in all probability he would die before Rory, but that made him object even more to the fact that the Trust was selling the title of the Retreat and the farmhouse to Rory even before he was dead. Especially since the Trust was lending Rory and Valerie the money to buy the Retreat and the house.

Bob Henry took Mike's objections remarkably calmly. He said he was sure the Retreat was an excellent investment. He had, he told Mike, been consulting with the Chakra Healer, Daintree Simpson, at the Retreat. She had done wonders for him. And even more for his wife. His married life had never been better, if Mike knew what he meant. Nudge, nudge; wink, wink. Mike should try it himself. Take Mary up there. He was sure Rory would give them mate's rates.

Mike had no intention of visiting Rory and no intention of letting him know that his cancer may not have been cured. In fact, Mike decided, he wouldn't even let the oncologist know that his cancer might have returned. He recalled his plan to move north, away from the city, away from oncologists and pathologists and waiting rooms. He would call Damian and discuss what renovations he thought would make the house saleable. Then, after the end of term and the school play, he and Mary would disappear.

But in the meantime, there was still the problem of the outstanding blood test.

Mike consulted the books on prostate cancer that the oncologist had given him several years earlier. There was a segment on PSA readings after the discontinuation of hormone treatment. Some patients, long-term, still had near zero PSA Readings, but everybody, both the cured and the uncured, showed an initial increase in their PSA rate for a year or so; moving up to about 2 or 3 in surviving patients, then falling back. Mike wanted one of those readings so the oncologist would give him some peace.

He'd read of sportspeople who cheated drug tests by getting somebody else to take the test. It seemed quite a simple idea. Anybody with a request form from an oncologist or a GP could go into a pathology lab and get a test, provided they had the real patient's identity cards and knew their address and date of birth and had a similar medical history so that the results wouldn't be too different.

That's when Mike remembered John Maguire.

Like Mike he'd had prostate cancer and radiation treatment.

Had he had hormone treatment?

Was his PSA normal?

The nurses had confused the two of them before. Was there a way to confuse them again?

Mike went looking for John Maguire on Facebook, Twitter and other social media.

He wasn't hard to find.

He was a writer and seemingly not a very successful one, given that on Facebook for example, he only had a few dozen friends and quite a few of those had no I.D. photo and only seemed to post highly flattering critiques of his books; so flattering that it made Mike think that they might actually have been written by John Maguire himself using pseudonyms.

Mike read John's latest book; a book that convinced Mike that John was an intelligent man, but not half as smart as he thought he was.

The book was about the need of all men, except the author of course, to believe in a God. Written in the first person it involved a man who decides that, to give people what they need, and to make a lot of tax-free money, he would start his own religion. He starts by joining a fringe

Evangelical Christian group and contesting and challenging the pontifications of their leader to such a degree that he eventually becomes an alternative leader and sets up his own church with its own tax-free status. Adored and revered by his few followers, especially the buxom young women, he eventually starts to believe his own publicity, and when a terrorist strikes in a nearby shopping centre, he steps up to confront him; certain that he is immortal and can talk the terrorist down.

He can't and he is shot dead, thus becoming a martyr and a much greater religious leader in death than he had ever been in life. Although, since it was written in the first person, it is the author himself who is telling you that in death he has become a God, thus suggesting that he has beaten death itself; as all Gods do.

Mike decided that anybody who could write a book like that had to be incredibly vain, and anybody so vain could easily be persuaded that they could get away with taking a blood test in somebody else's name. He contacted John on Messenger and told him a story, largely based on truth:

Mike was a teacher. He had read John's book. He thought the book raised many interesting questions and he would like his class to read and discuss the book and maybe even get John to come into the school for a question and answer session.

John's reply came before Mike had even logged off and they arranged to meet in a small inner-city café near the fourth-floor, no-lift, bedsitter, where John lived and worked.

From the start John was only interested in getting his book into Mike's School. Meeting the students. Showing them how smart he was. Mike was only interested in getting John to take his blood test for him, provided of course that John's PSA was not rising as quickly as his.

Finding this out was no problem. Mike just asked him how his treatment was going and John just couldn't stop talking about himself. He complained about how long the treatment had taken; completely ignoring the fact that Mike had undergone similar treatment. He complained that the doctors behaved as if they were Gods. It was a common theme of John's thinking.

Mike sympathized with him. He was having the same problem. Even after all this time his oncologist was trying to get him back on to hormone therapy; just because his PSA had risen back above 2.

"Two isn't high, is it?" Mike appealed to John.

"Tell him to get stuffed," said John, getting into the swing of the thing.

"I would," said Mike, "But the wife..."

John nodded as if he knew what Mike was talking about, even though he no longer had a wife, having already lost two.

Then Mike appeared to have just thought of something, although he'd thought of it long before he'd even gotten in touch with John.

"How's your PSA?" he asked.

"1.6 last time I checked."

"Do you want to check it again?"

"Not for another six months," said John. "I hate it as much as you do. Especially the follow up meeting with the oncologist."

"Take my test," Mike suggested. "That way you can check it without your oncologist knowing it was you, so you won't have to see him. And I can show my wife my PSA is below three, get her and my oncologist off my back. Stop them all from trying to play God."

John hesitated. How could he take Mike's test?

"Easy," said Mike, "We look alike, I could give you my driving license, my date of birth, my Medicare card, a sample of my signature, although they never check it."

John still hesitated but Mike ploughed on.

"I could give you my pathology test request when I come to collect the books," he said.

It was the books that distracted John, as Mike knew they would.

"What books?" he asked.

"I'll need to buy at least forty copies so the class can read them before you meet for the Q&A," Mike said, "I assume you can get hold of forty copies? We'd pay for them, of course."

"Yeah," John nodded, "I can probably get hold of forty copies."

In fact, his publisher had had so many returns on the run of five hundred copies that they'd initially printed, that John could probably have gotten hold of ten times that number.

He was in a bind. The more he thought about it, the less he liked the idea of taking a blood test in Mike's name. But getting his book into a classroom, maybe even onto a school syllabus; that was the dream, the Holy Grail, and John knew he was going to take the test.

In fact, he even shaved his beard and had his hair cut so that he looked more like Mike in his driving licence photo. And Mike, in turn, started growing a beard and letting his hair grow to look more like John, in preparation for his journey north.

The first Mary learnt of Mike's renewed interest in selling the house and moving to Queensland was when Mike arrived home with Damian Koh and another member of the golf club, a builder named Marty. Together they moved through the house, pointing out the flaws, suggesting the remedies. Each job was fairly small but the costs started to mount up.

"Are you sure we can afford all this?" asked Mary.

"Not a problem, Mrs. Maguire," said Damian. "You can pay me when the house is sold."

Mary still wasn't satisfied. She turned back to Mike.

"What about your blood tests? What if your PSA is still rising? You'll have to stay in Sydney for treatment."

"Okay," said Mike, "We'll delay the renovations until we get my next blood tests back. If they're okay, then we'll start work."

Mary still looked reluctant.

"Don't worry," said Mike, "If the PSA says I'm fine, we've got nothing to worry about for years. And I'm sure there are oncologists in Queensland."

Which left Mary in the same position as John. She had no choice but to go along with Mike's plan. But again, like John, she had no idea of the true extent of Mike's scheming.

CHAPTER NINE

T he New Year brought a kind of Indian Summer into the lives of both Mike and Rory.

Mike's production of the school play was a huge success, made more special by the cast singing a song of farewell to Mike after the curtain call. For the first time since their now grownup son Matthew was born, Mary saw Mike cry.

The house sold for a couple of hundred thousand dollars more than the reserve and, with the extra money, Mike insisted that Matthew, his daughter-in-law Charlotte and his grandson, Lucas, accompany him and Mary north to search for their new home.

They stayed in a four-star resort in Cairns but the type of house Mike was insisting on buying wasn't necessarily four-star. He was only interested in the most isolated and private of properties, regardless of comfort or condition. Hopefully where no interfering oncologist could find him.

Mathew had always been protective of his mother, so eventually, with his help, they managed to meet both Mike and Mary's needs by finding a large and well maintained homestead, with outbuildings, on its own land; secluded, surrounded by native forest and bordered by a river but not too far from the nearest small town with a primary school, which was in need of teachers. All for more than half a million dollars less than they'd got for their Sydney home.

Mary thought the house was perfect but she was still a

little concerned about the location. The local town had no secondary school; nowhere for Mike to work.

"No worries, said Mike, "I'm not going back to teaching. I'll write that book, maybe start up a little business of my own. Maybe something in tourism or agriculture."

Mary knew Mike knew nothing about tourism or agriculture but she didn't fret. If they started to run short of money Mike could always get a teaching job in Cairns. The commute would be no greater than the commute they both used to make in Sydney. You can cover a lot of territory in half an hour in the bush. Besides, Mike had offered Matthew a hundred thousand dollars as a loan to put towards the deposit on a house in Sydney.

Matthew tried to refuse but Mike insisted, even though they both knew Matthew would probably never be able to pay his parents back. Feeling quite emotional, Mike said that Matthew would be doing him a favour if he took the money. When Mike thought he was going to die, he explained, the one thing that bothered him was that he wouldn't leave Mary and Matthew financially secure. Now he could do that. He could face death with equanimity; not that he was intended to die, of course, he should add. Matthew hugged his father. Mary hugged them both. Charlotte and a rather confused Lucas joined in and it ended up as a huge family group hug.

Having secured the future for his family, Mike really got the spending bug. He insisted on buying a four-wheel drive campervan and a boat that was so heavy that he had to buy a manual fork-lift to get it on and off the campervan's roof when he went camping. He bought a trail bike, although he'd never ridden a bike in his life. And he bought a commercial freezer big enough to store a two-metre shark, even though he only bought light fishing tackle for fresh water fishing. Matthew was convinced his dad didn't need these things and would never use them.

To prove Matthew wrong, Mike insisted on taking the entire family, including young Lucas, on a camping expedition into the Daintree Rainforest. It was magical. Only spoilt by signs everywhere, warning about crocodiles. Nevertheless the warnings were taken seriously, the tent was eschewed and everybody crammed into the campervan to sleep that night.

The next morning they used the fork-lift to get the boat off of the campervan roof and into the water, to take Matthew and Lucas fishing. The fishing wasn't without incident. They'd hardly cast their lines into the water when they became aware that the crocodiles sunning themselves on the riverbank were as long as the boat they were sitting in. In fact, when one of them slipped into the water, it was obvious that it was actually longer than the boat.

Matthew was terrified but he didn't want to show fear in front of his son. Maybe he could persuade Lucas to say he wanted to go back to the camping ground?

"Are you all right, Luke?" he asked his seven-year-old son.

The boy turned to his father; his face aglow.

"It's exciting," he said, "It makes me hot under my skin."

Matthew could hardly suggest they leave after that, but he wasn't happy.

"Don't worry," Mike told Mathew, "Have you ever heard of anybody being taken from a boat in the Daintree?"

"Have you ever heard of anybody fishing in a boat this small in the Daintree?" Matthew countered; but they remained moored where they were, and while Matthew gripped onto an oar and watched the nearby crocodiles carefully, Mike and Lucas fished.

Luke even caught a couple of good-sized trevally, which made Matthew even more nervous, afraid one of the crocodiles might decide to follow the fish into the boat.

Eventually, with the sun dropping low on the horizon, Mike started the outboard and they returned to the jetty at the camping site, where Mary prepared barbecued fish and salad for dinner.

Luke declared it *'the best day, ever.'* While Matthew insisted on keeping the fire burning brightly; supposedly because it was getting cold but everyone knew it was to ward off the crocodiles. He came in for some good-natured ribbing from his father over it, but when push came to shove, Mike also decided to sleep safely inside the campervan again, along with everyone else.

In fact, they never even unpacked the tent the whole time they were there.

Things were going equally well for Rory. The Retreat opened with little fanfare but it slowly gained a regular and loyal clientele. Enough, if not to make Rory rich, at least to enable him to comfortably make the payments on the enormous loans he had taken out to acquire the Retreat and the farmhouse.

Both Valerie and Rory really got into the spirit of playing hosts. Rory certainly looked the part, letting his hair grow, wearing a large crystal around his neck and rings on his fingers. But he was wise enough to restrict his involvement in the Retreat to greeting the guests when they first arrived, and topping up the glass of the occasional corporate visitor.

Valerie too, was only interested in the money, but Daintree showed a real talent for Chakra Healing and guiding people on a path of discovery. So much so, in fact, that the Retreat became two businesses in one: a luxury corporate bolt hole where stressed executives could indulge themselves; and a genuine Retreat, or more precisely a series of retreats, run by Daintree.

The Executives arrived at the weekends. The retreats were held during the week. Sometimes for women only. Sometimes for men only. Sometimes even for couples. Bob Henry and his wife had been guests at these retreats, although not together. Even so, as Bob had told Mike, their marriage had never been better.

Everything seemed to be going smoothly for everybody... until six months after John Maguire had taken Mike's blood test. Just around the time that the world started hearing reports of a new SARS-like virus appearing in China. But all this seemed far away for the time being and had little effect on Mike and Mary.

Mary had settled in well at her new school. She was surprised to find that she actually preferred the unspoilt country kids to the kids from the more stressed suburbs of her previous school. The parents were a lot more easy-going, too. And very friendly. They were always inviting Mary along to social gatherings and local sporting events. Mary did her best to fit in and make friends but it was a bit difficult without Mike.

He seemed to have taken on the life of a hermit, and a pretty self-sufficient hermit at that. The property already had the ubiquitous array of tropical fruit trees when they'd bought it, but Mike had added a vegetable patch, a greenhouse, and a cultivated area of the forest where, just outside his actual property, under the rainforest trees, he grew a very successful, not inconsiderable, crop of marijuana.

Mary worried about it, but Mike laughed it off.

"Nobody's going to complain about a few plants for personal use," he said, "especially for a cancer survivor."

He did feel the odd twinge and occasionally passed blood, but the Surgeon had said that this was to be expected after the brachia treatment and radiology band therapy. Nevertheless, Mike was still careful to hide it from Mary. He told himself he didn't want to worry her for nothing. The truth was he didn't want Mary panicking and insisting he visit the oncologist.

In the end, his efforts were in vain because Mary didn't need to contact the oncologist; the oncologist contacted Mike, insisting that it was time for another check-up. Mike, quite reasonably said that he didn't want to go travelling two and a half thousand kilometres by road from Cairns to Sydney just to have a blood test. The Sydney oncologist sent up the name of a colleague in Cairns, along with a note explaining that he had passed on Mike's case files and he was enclosing a blood test referral. Mike stuck the letter and the blood test referral onto the corkboard in the kitchen and prepared to head off on a lone fishing expedition in the Daintree.

"You're not putting the blood tests off," Mary insisted.

Mike took her by the shoulders and looked straight into her eyes.

"I'm not putting anything off. Promise. I'll handle it as soon as I get back." he said, although he had no intention at all of contacting the Cairns oncologist.

Mike went camping and fishing in the Daintree quite often. He had made friends with an indigenous Park Ranger named Warren Hodgson. Warren had taken Mike under his wing and taught him not only how to fish but how to recognize plants and animals in the rainforest.

He even took him along whenever a particularly large crocodile was causing concern and showed him how they trapped the animals and transferred them to crocodile parks across Queensland and the Northern Territory.

It was useless, Warren told Mike, trapping the crocodiles and releasing them a few hundred miles up the coast. Sooner or later, the crocodiles would make their way back home to the river and Warren would have to repeat the process. And a crocodile that had already been caught and released was even more difficult, and dangerous, to catch a second time.

Not that they had to catch many crocs. It took a long time for a croc to grow sufficiently to be considered a danger on the river. Even then the Rangers tended to leave them in place until they started causing trouble. By taking a dog maybe, or a bite out of somebody's boat.

There were plenty of big crocs still on the river and Mike started to recognise each one by name. He was particularly fond of a large croc named Humphrey; although it was a fondness tinged with fear and a warning from Warren. Humphrey had been watching Mike fish, and knew that Mike, like all good fishermen, threw most of his catch back into the water. And when he did, Humphrey was there, looking for a free feed.

Mike tried varying his routine. Holding on to all the fish for just one release. Releasing them as soon as he caught them. Whatever he did, sooner or later Humphrey would appear. In the end, Mike took to releasing fish he didn't want as he went, then taking the last of his unwanted catch downstream, away from his camp, before releasing them into the water. That way, he reasoned, even if Humphrey followed him, he'd lose interest once the fish were jettisoned, and wouldn't follow him back to the camping ground.

Mike wasn't the only one having a few nervous moments. Mary had mixed feelings about living in such an isolated place when Mike was away. Mike had tried to allay her fear by installing motion activated lights around the house.

Initially that just made things worse.

There were a lot of animals roaming around the house that were more than large enough to activate the lights. Possums, kangaroos, even large birds like cassowaries. The result was that the lights were always turning on and Mary was always peering out the window, nervously looking for intruders. Eventually Mary employed a bit of lateral thinking to solve this problem. She put out food for the kangaroos and possums. That way she knew the lights would be turned on and the house would be bathed in enough light all the time to hopefully dissuade any would-be human intruders.

One night while Mike was away, before Mary had had time to put food out for the wildlife, the outside lights suddenly switched on.

Mary looked out nervously, then her pulse rate returned to normal as she saw Mike's silhouette through the glass door.

Then her pulse rate rose again when the man didn't walk in, as Mike would have done, but instead tapped loudly on the glass.

Mary opened the glass door, but only after locking the fly-wire door.

Mary looked at the man. He looked like Mike, but he wasn't Mike.

"Who are you?" she demanded, clutching the large

knife that she had been using to cut vegetables.

The man, for all his dishevelled looks, looked positively terrified.

"John," he said, "John Maguire. I'm Mike's cousin. Is he home?"

Mike had never mentioned that he had a cousin, so Mary didn't let her guard down immediately.

"He will be soon," she said, trying to warn her visitor not to try anything.

John relaxed; tried his best to look friendly.

"Good. Can I wait inside?"

He glanced around nervously.

"I'm an inner-city boy," he said, "Live in Balmain. All this emptiness makes me jumpy"

He peered out into the darkness beyond the house-lights and gave a little smile.

"I hear you even have man-killing birds up here?"

"Cassowaries," Mary agreed.

She looked at him. He looked harmless enough. And nervous enough. She unlocked the fly-wire door and stood back to let him in. He was carrying a duffle bag which he held up.

"Mike said I could stay a couple of nights, while we settle some business," he said.

"What business?"

John hesitated.

"I'd rather not say,"

Which made Mary question whether she was wise to have let him in.

Having John in the house was very disconcerting. Not just because he looked so much like Mike but because he was so mysterious, and he even acted like Mike.

Mary put him in the annex where young Lucas slept

on family visits. There was a separate bathroom and bedroom in there and even though there was only a single
bed, Mary didn't think John would mind. From his appearance he looked like he might have slept rough a few
times.

When he emerged from his bedroom it was even
more disconcerting. He had showered and changed into
the Steve Irwin-esque type khaki short-sleeved shirt and
shorts that Mike had affected ever since the move north.
To make matters worse, John insisted on helping get dinner and he was about as useless as Mike. In the end Mary
had to get him to set the table and pour the wine because
he just got in the way doing anything else.

Predictably, he set the table with his setting exactly
where Mike usually sat. He did things so like Mike, acted
like him, sounded like him, that it seemed they must have
spent their lives together. Yet in over thirty years, Mike
had never even mentioned a cousin, let alone introduced
her to one.

Mary had to ask how exactly John and Mike were re-
lated.

"We're cousins," John repeated, "On our dads' side."

"Mike's never mentioned you," said Mary.

John grinned in the same self-effacing manner that
Mike often grinned.

"Yeah, well," he said, "I don't think Mike even knows
I am his cousin. I did a search when I first met him.
You know? Through Ancestry.com? Turns out our fathers
were brothers. They were both put in an orphanage, then
separated. Both ended up in Sydney. But they never actually kept in touch."

This sounded right. Mary didn't know a family as anti-
social as Mike's.

"So where did you and Mike meet?" she asked.

"We both had prostate cancer at the same time," said John, "The nurses often confused us. I wonder whether Mike didn't get my treatment at times, and vice versa."

John offered no further explanation and Mary had to push.

"So, you became friends then?"

"No," said John, "In fact, I didn't even notice Mike during the radiotherapy sessions. You're a bit out of it, getting that treatment. This fish is very good."

They had just started eating, but it seemed to Mary that John added this last remark in order to change the subject. Which, of course made Mary even keener to pursue it.

"So how did you become friends?" she asked and when he hesitated, added more bluntly, "What are you doing here?"

"Well," said John, "I promised Mike I'd come up."

"Why?" demanded Mary.

John shrugged.

"I'm a writer. Mike read my book, offered to get it into his class as a study book. Get me in to talk to the kids. Very interesting. Really makes you think why you wrote what you wrote, with a set of smart kids asking questions."

"Mike isn't teaching now," Mary said.

"No," agreed John, "I spoke to the kids in Sydney. I think it really helped me as a writer."

"And you've come all this way to say thank you," Mary said sarcastically, tired of John's obfuscation.

"Well, no," said John, "Mike did me a real favour getting me into the school. Sales of the book have really picked up. I said I'd do Mike a favour in return."

"What favour?" asked Mary.

"If Mike hasn't told you, I don't think I should," said John, and he suddenly took a deep interest in his salad.

Mary just glared at him in silence. And the silence continued, and would have continued for even longer if they hadn't heard the sound of Mike's campervan engine as he drove up and parked beside the house.

CHAPTER TEN

G rand Deceptions don't work unless they are preceded by smaller deceptions. All the players need to be compromised; committed to the Grand Deception in order to hide their own smaller secrets.

Rory and Valerie started it by pretending to the bank that they owned the farm.

Bob Henry added to the deceptions by supporting the Retreat, at possibly great and unjustified expense to the Trust, simply because Daintree caused strange movements in his nether region that he thought he would never experience again. His deception may not have been actually illegal, but it was certainly unethical.

Daintree might be accused of being deceptive, but if she were, the main person she deceived was herself. She thought that she really had become a healer and guru in ten weeks. She believed it. The attendees at the Retreat believed it. And given that there are no formal qualifications for Shamanism, who is to say she hadn't, in a remarkably short time, achieved enlightenment. Certainly, nobody could question the sincerity of her beliefs or the ethicality of her actions, apart from putting Viagra powder in Bob Henry's drink, of course.

Mike, too, was guilty. If he hadn't persuaded, well, *bribed* John Maguire to take his PSA test, then John wouldn't have had any part in the story.

And without John, there would have been no Grand Deception.

In many ways Mike and John were polar opposites, despite being connected by blood, .

Mike had always claimed he wanted to write a book but never had the time.

John had never wanted to write a book but found himself with no other visible means of support.

He had been a journalist. More specifically, he had been a columnist. He did big exposes and he wrote opinion pieces. The problem was John's opinions didn't always agree with those of the Media Baron he worked for.

When he wrote pieces about animal cruelty, he got away with it. He even managed to post his counter-view concerning global warming. But when Donald Trump was elected President of The United States of America, John used up the last of his nine lives. He wrote a piece, backed by direct quotes and factual reports, basically saying that when John was a child a "trump" was a small fart, and as far as he could see nothing much had changed.

Inevitably, when the next set of redundancies arrived at the newspaper, John's name was at the top of the list. He was just one of many, but everybody knew why he had been laid off. Furthermore, nobody else in the Media Empire would employ him, and the Media Empire owned most of the newspapers in Australia.

So John decided to write a book. It wasn't just about the need all people seemed to have to believe in a God but also about the people who sought to set themselves up as Gods or the Messengers of Gods. People who, by definition, were opinionated and greedy, and were often sexual predators and paedophiles to boot: people who often attained high office in the various churches and the media.

The book didn't sell well until Mike made it a classroom text to study.

John used this information, with a slight exaggeration

and omission-

"The book has been used as a Grade Ten text in NSW,"
– to get the book into a few local libraries and get a few old colleagues on newspapers to review it. No mention that it was only one class in one school. Added to the on-line reviews that John wrote himself, under pseudonyms, (just another small deception) it was enough to turn the book into a minor success.

Soon he had sufficient funds to buy an old car from a man in the pub, although he didn't bother to change the registration, to avoid paying stamp duty. He also forgot to renew his driving licence, which had expired while he was undergoing treatment for the cancer. So, he was driving a car registered in somebody else's name, while technically he was an unlicensed driver. Despite this, he went looking for news stories which, if they were sensational enough, he could sell as a freelancer.

One of John's pet hates was animal cruelty. He had worked on the live sheep story, the export of greyhounds' story and the selling racehorses for dogfood story. So, when he received a tip-off that an abattoir in southern Queensland was again turning slow horses into fast profits as pet food, despite having no registration or a driving licence, John headed north to investigate.

Since Australians had only recently become aware of a new Corona Virus making an appearance in China people weren't taking it seriously as yet. Certainly, they hadn't closed the New South Wales/ Queensland border as they would later do.

John slipped into Queensland un-noticed, via Tenterfield and the New England Highway.

He knew stories sold a lot better with video footage so his first task was to set up remote cameras in the abattoir above the yards and the slaughter room. He chose a night with no moon, but despite this he hadn't even installed the first camera when he heard voices and footsteps.

Standing stock still on the railings above the yard in total darkness did him no good.

The abattoir lights suddenly came on.

Somebody raised a shot-gun in John's direction and fired. He jumped down into the horse yards where he narrowly avoided being trampled to death by a herd of frightened thoroughbreds each weighing around five hundred kilograms.

He could hear people yelling. There was more than one of them. They seemed to have him surrounded. One of the voices mentioned the stock in the stockyards. John was about to be caught and since his would-be captors were prepared to shoot at him, he wasn't expecting any gentle treatment.

There was only one thing to do.

He unlocked the yard gate and yelled and slapped at the frightened horses milling around him. They weren't waiting to be told twice. They bolted out of the yard, first a couple, then a torrent.

The first gunman approaching the yard was too slow. The lead horse barrelled into him and he clattered against the yard railings.

Whether he was hurt or dead, John had no idea, and didn't intend to hang about to find out. As men yelled and tried to either corral or evade the fleeing horses, John joined the stampede as the horses ran out onto the street. Hidden amongst the horses, John ran for his car, parked a few hundred yards away.

He jumped into the car, panting heavily. He turned the ignition. It wouldn't start. He was flooding it. He composed himself, counted to ten, then tried the ignition again and this time it started. He roared off at high speed, ignoring a couple of shotgun blasts behind him. Neither made contact with the car.

John had always fancied himself as a good driver and his only consideration now was to head south as quickly as possible. Out of Queensland, over the border and on to Tenterfield where he'd booked a room for the night.

The road wasn't busy. John could sit on a hundred and ten without difficulty. That is, until he heard the familiar wail, and saw the flashing blue light coming up fast, behind him.

For a brief moment John considered trying to out-run the police-car but it was a long, straight, open road and the police-car was closing fast. John had no option but to pull over.

John was generally good in an emergency, or so he thought. After all, he'd kept himself alive in several theatres of war when he'd worked as a war correspondent. He knew he had real problems. Driving without a license. Speeding. Trespass back at the abattoir. Possibly attempted murder by horse, and certainly intention to do grievous bodily harm and causing an affray by releasing a herd of terrified horses onto the roads of Queensland.

Despite this, he remained reasonably calm as he wound down his window and waited for the young police officer to approach the vehicle. He suspected that all the policeman knew at this point was that he had been speeding. With a bit of luck he wouldn't yet be connected to the ruckus at the abattoir. It was too soon after the event.

"Do you know what speed you were doing, sir?" the young officer asked.

This was good. No questions about where he'd been.

"Yes, sorry Officer," John said, "I'm booked into a motel in Tenterfield tonight. I was probably speeding a little to get there before they close the office."

"Perhaps you should settle for a room in Stanthorpe?" said the officer, "It's a lot closer. Can I see your licence please, sir?"

John pretended to check his wallet, his pockets.

"Sorry, Officer, I don't seem to be able to find it."

"You know that's an offence, not carrying your licence?" the officer said, "and there's an on the spot fine for speeding."

"Happy to pay it in cash," said John, "and I can give you my details: name, date of birth, address?"

The officer took out his charge sheet to write out a speeding infringement. The man was going to pay. The officer would get his revenue target up for the month. He wasn't really interested in John's identity, but he asked for his details anyway.

John didn't hesitate.

"Michael Maguire, born November the eleventh, nineteen sixty-five. Fifteen Scales Road, Chatswood, New South Wales."

It was six months since John had taken the blood test for Mike, but he was a good reporter. He remembered details, and the signature he wrote on the speeding fine was also a reasonable facsimile of Mike's signature.

"Drive carefully," said the officer, "And if you're not going to make Tenterfield tonight, stop at Stanthorpe."

"Thank you, Officer," said John, and as the officer returned to his patrol car, John turned on his car ignition and drove smoothly off down the road.

The police car followed him for a while but he was just making sure John didn't resume speeding. When the police car pulled off to the side of the road, John eventually relaxed. The adrenalin release made him burst out laughing.

Back at his Tenterfield motel, John made a few phone calls and filed his story about a shooting at an abattoir in Queensland where they were slaughtering ex-racehorses. His phone calls to the local Queensland hospital had revealed that one of the men had a broken leg, another had crushed ribs. John even had the nerve to call the local police station and asked if they'd arrested anybody; either the employees at the abattoir for firing their shotguns, or the animal rights activist they had been trying to shoot? When John was ready to file the story, he was careful to insist that he didn't get a by-line; asking instead that the papers attributed it to *'our Queensland reporter'*. He then got mildly drunk before turning in for the night. The shooting story had been better than any pictures of horses milling around or animal cruelty. He was very pleased.

Then, in the middle of the night, he suddenly sat bolt upright and stared at the wall. Obviously, the police would be looking for the animal rights activist. It wouldn't be hard to tie in his car fleeing the scene. He needed to sell the car, using the previous owners' registration papers and selling it for cash. But first he had to get to Mike Maguire before the police did and make sure that when they asked if there was anybody who knew his birthday and his address, and could copy his signature, Mike wouldn't mention him.

Which is why he now sat waiting, as Mike came in from his trip to the Daintree.

CHAPTER ELEVEN

Mike walked into the house and stopped. He hadn't expected to see John, who was already getting to his feet and moving to greet him.

"John," Mike said, "What are you doing here?"

Mary hadn't moved from her chair.

"He's come to do you a favour," she said.

Mike looked at her, confused. Then he looked at John, confused.

"The blood test," said John, in a stage whisper that came out rather louder than he intended. He cleared his throat, "Er..I just got my reminder."

"Ah, forget about that," said Mike. "I'm not having any more tests."

"Yes, you are," insisted Mary.

"I'm not," said Mike.

He headed for the fridge and got himself a beer.

John looked at Mary, not sure how to proceed. Then he looked at Mike.

"Could I talk to you in private?" he asked.

Mike shrugged and took a swig of the beer.

"Sure," he said, "You can help me put the fish I caught into the freezer."

And he put down the beer and walked back out to the campervan.

John followed him, casting a nervous look over his shoulder to see if Mary was following.

She wasn't. She just sat there… arms folded.

A couple of hours later, Mary got into bed, folded her arms

again… and waited.

Mike pretended he didn't know what was going on and got into bed, seemingly unconcerned. He switched off his bedside light, puffed his pillow and lay down with his back to Mary.

Mary didn't move. She still sat upright. She still left her bedside light switched on.

Eventually Mike knew he had no alternative but to come clean.

"John took my last blood test for me," he said, his eyes still closed. "My PSA was rising a bit. I didn't want to take any chances that the oncologist would insist that I go back on hormone treatment."

Mary was astounded.

"You cheated on your blood test? You lied to me?"

"No," Mike insisted, sitting up with a sigh, "The PSA was just a little bit up. Trouble is, now if I take the blood test the PSA would have gone up, gone down, and then gone up again. They're bound to insist on more tests and treatment 'just in case'. So, John has to take my test again."

"There is no way that man is taking your blood test again," said Mary. "And you can tell the oncologist the truth if you don't want more tests."

"Mary," Mike protested.

"No," she said, "Either you take the test or I tell the oncologist what you've done. I'm sure it's against the law. This is your health we're talking about… your life."

Mike reluctantly agreed.

"Oh, all right," he said and turned his back on Mary, supposedly to go to sleep.

Mary seemed to follow suit. She puffed up her pillow, turned off her light, almost got her head onto the pillow, then sat back up again, switched the light on again.

"There is no way he's driven two thousand kilometres to take a blood test for you. Not when you didn't even ask him to."

Mike reluctantly sat up again. He'd told Mary the worst part of the story. He might as well tell her the rest. John had been caught speeding, he explained; driving a car that wasn't registered in his name, without a license. He had been doing an undercover story on an abattoir that was slaughtering racehorses. Somebody got hurt. The police would be looking for John, so he gave them Mike's name.

Knowing how fond of animals Mary was, Mike put a lot of emphasis on the cruelty of the abattoir that John was trying to expose; was successfully exposing actually. Just about every news source was taking the story.

Mary wasn't fooled.

"The abattoir has nothing to do with the fact that he gave the police your name. That was down to John entirely. He could have given any old name."

"The police have computers these days, they can check things really fast," said Mike. "If he'd given a made-up name, they might have arrested him on the spot."

"Serves him right," said Mary.

"Look," said Mike, "It's no problem for us if he used my name. I've got an alibi. I was up in the Daintree with Warren Hodgson when John was pulled over. Warren will back me up."

"So, you're going to lie for him now?" Mary said, "You're bloody soft. You know that? No wonder your brother and sister-in-law have stolen your father's Trust from under your nose and you've done nothing about it."

"They haven't stolen the Trust," said Mike, taken aback.

"No? If Rory dies, will you get the farmhouse and the

Retreat, or will they stay with Valerie?"

Mike didn't answer.

"That's most of the bloody Trust," said Mary, and this time she did switch off her light and turn her back on Mike. And it was Mike who was left sitting up, staring into the darkness.

It wasn't true that the farmhouse and the Retreat were most of the Trust, but they were a substantial part of it. That in itself didn't particularly bother Mike. What bothered Mike was that his wife thought he had been robbed and had been too soft to do anything about it. It bothered him, but not enough for him to do anything about it. Bugger them, he thought. He didn't need them. He lay down, closed his eyes, exhausted by the fishing expedition; ready for sleep.

No such luck. Mary was sitting up again. The bedside light was coming on again.

"What about the car?" Mary demanded.

"What car?" Mike groaned.

" *His* car. The police must have his registration number. If they come here to check on your licence, they'll see it."

Mike didn't sit up. He didn't even open his eyes.

"I'll put it in the shed," he muttered.

"No, you won't," said Mary, "That's the first place they'll look. Hide it in the bush somewhere. Deep in the bush."

"Okay," said Mike, and turned over in bed. "I'll hide it in the marijuana plantation."

"Oh, great," said Mary. "Now you'll get booked for speeding, breaking into an abattoir *and* cultivating an illegal substance."

But Mike just lay there, snoring gently. Mary gave him a none too gentle shove in the back.

"Well, go on then," she said. "Tomorrow might be too

late."

As usual, Mary was right.

The following morning Mary, Mike and John were having breakfast when a police car drove into the yard. John immediately bolted for Lucas's bedroom at the far end of the house, taking his breakfast plate and his cup of tea with him.

Mike walked out on to the verandah to greet the police.

"Morning," he said, "Can I help you?"

"Michael Maguire?" the policeman asked, "Michael Maguire of 15, Scales Street, Chatswood. New South Wales"

"Yes," said Mike, "Well, I used to live there. I live here now... Just me and Mary."

Mary, listening from the kitchen table, thought the added information he offered made him sound guilty but the policeman didn't seem to notice.

"You should get a Queensland licence," he said.

"Yeah, I've been meaning to," said Mike.

"Can I see your New South Wales licence, please?" asked the policeman.

'Sure, " said Mike, and pretended to rummage around for it, but he knew exactly where he'd put his wallet: on the kitchen bench.

Eventually he 'found' it, gave Mary a nervous look and handed the licence to the policeman, who had followed him inside.

Mary was still sitting impassively at the table. She'd spent the morning looking up reports of the fracas at the abattoir. Nobody had been killed. The abattoir had been temporarily closed down by Queensland Health. John really had achieved something. That didn't mean Mary forgave him for involving Mike. Or forgave Mike for getting John to take his blood test.

The policeman handed back Mike's licence after checking it.

"Can you tell us where you were going the night before last, Mr. Maguire?" the policeman asked.

"Night before last?" Mike repeated, "I was up in the Daintree, fishing."

"You weren't on the Warwick-Stanhope road, speeding?"

"No," said Mike, "I was up in the Daintree. Warren Hodgson, the Park Ranger up there, he'll back me up."

"Just one moment," said the policeman, and he went back to his car to radio in this new information.

"Now you're in trouble for not getting a Queensland licence," said Mary.

"Have you changed your licence over yet?" Mike snapped back.

"No," said Mary, "And if I get in trouble for that, that'll be your fault, too."

The policeman returned a second time.

"Somebody gave your name and address in New South Wales and your date of birth to Highway Patrol, just north of Stanhope. We believe the individual may have been involved in an incident at an abattoir near there."

Mike shrugged, "I don't know anything about that."

"Is that where they were slaughtering racehorses?" asked Mary, "I read about it on the internet."

"That's right, Madam," said the policeman, and he turned back to Mike.

"Do you know anybody who knows your old address and date of birth and who looks like you? You fit the description given by the highway patrolman. Anybody who might give your name if he were stopped for speeding?"

"No," said Mike.

"There's your brother, Rory," put in Mary. "If he was caught speeding, he wouldn't be above using your name."

"Why would he?" Mike frowned.

"Maybe he's got points on his licence," Mary shrugged. "Maybe another speeding fine would have meant he lost his licence. He'd give your name then. I can't see him being involved in the abattoir fracas, though., she continued. "Rory doesn't give a shit about anybody but himself."

"Where does he live, this Rory?" the policeman asked.

"Northern New South Wales. Not far from Stanhope." said Mary, helpfully.

"Address?"

"The Golden Topaz Retreat," said Mary, "Near Federal."

The policeman took down the information, returned to his police car and drove off.

After a moment, John re-emerged still carrying his breakfast.

"Thanks," he said.

"Don't mention it," Mary said, "Anytime I can make life difficult for my brother-in-law, I'm always happy to do it."

Which was unfortunate for Rory, because events meant Mary was about to be in a position to make life very difficult indeed; for him and Valerie.

CHAPTER TWELVE

As it was around the world, the initial reaction to the Coronavirus in Australia was pretty lackadaisical.

Among the first actions taken was a ban on all crowds at football matches… although the ban wasn't going to take place until the following Monday. Then the Prime Minister totally undercut the cautionary message by saying he was going to the footie on Sunday, no matter what. In the end he didn't go, but the damage had been done.

People still went to the footie; people gathered on Bondi Beach and ate at restaurants.

That is until they couldn't.

The Government closed all bars, clubs, restaurants, sporting stadiums, and by extension Wellness Retreats. It's hard to social distance and give a full body massage at the same time.

Daintree Simpson immediately adjusted her business model by offering an on-line Yoga service by video but the returns weren't great. Valerie reacted by immediately sacking her two Thai employees and sending them home, and Rory spoke to the bank who told him that they were considering a six months moratorium on all loan repayments. Rory breathed a sigh of relief and crossed his fingers, hoping that the pandemic would be all but a dim memory by then and life would resume as normal.

The outstanding problem at the moment was the money that Rory and Valerie had borrowed from his father's Trust, and surely Bob Henry would also agree to a loan repayment moratorium, especially if they continued to give him free sessions with Daintree.

Normally that would have been true, but these were not normal times.

The Trust, like everybody else, was going through difficult times. Their main business was the construction company that old Paddy Maguire had built up over sixty years. It was primarily a spec-building business. They built large developments, not necessarily with any single buyer in mind. They sold units and apartments off the plan. Often, when the market was hot, they would use a slight change in the specifications on the plan as an excuse to return deposits given by potential buyers; then they would resell the property to somebody else at a higher price. They justified this underhand behaviour by saying that when the market wasn't hot, buyers who had put down a deposit before the building was complete, would often forfeit the deposit rather than buy the unit at the agreed price.

The market had been bad for a few years. The construction company had barely kept its head above water. It was only because the market had picked up in the last year or so that Bob was able to loan Rory and Valerie the money to buy shares in the farm and take possession of the Retreat and the farmhouse.

Even then, no money had changed hands. The Trust was the seller and the financer, so in a series of purely paper transactions, the Trust loaned the money to Rory and Valerie, then received the money back for the sale of the shares. There was, in reality, no money, just some very large monthly loan repayments which Valerie and Rory had struggled to pay back even before the Covid outbreak.

Now there was no way of paying it back. Still, Valerie

and Rory were convinced that Bob would give them a loan repayment moratorium just like the bank. After all Bob was a regular visitor to Daintree and the Retreat. Lately, even his wife had taken a short retreat; an exclusive one, for women only. So, it was a surprise - no, it was a shock when Rory and Valerie received a letter from the Trust's solicitor, not even from Bob himself, informing them that the Trust expected them to continue making their monthly repayments and that if they fell three months behind, the Trust would, as per the terms of their agreement, foreclose on the loans and repossess both the farmhouse and the Retreat. They would, furthermore, require vacant possession of both properties at that time. Bob wasn't just intent on sending them broke, it seemed, he was intent on making them homeless.

Valerie came up with what she thought was the obvious solution.

"Get that bitch Daintree, or whatever she calls herself, to talk to Bob Henry." she said, "She can twist him around her little finger."

So, Rory went trotting down through the macadamia plantation and the rainforest, to the Retreat.

He found Daintree giving an on-line class to clients, using a camera set up in front of the Centre. Rory didn't like to interrupt her. Partly because it would be bad for business, but mostly because she was demonstrating the Pelvic Rock Exercise and advising her viewers to make a determined effort to enjoy themselves and think of Elvis Presley or Michael Jackson.

Rory could watch Daintree demonstrating the Pelvic Rock Exercise for hours, and he probably would have, if Valerie hadn't appeared and unceremoniously pulled the plug on the video camera.

"It's all right," she said, "They'll think it was a power outage or they'll blame the NBN."

She didn't bother with any further preamble, getting straight to the point.

"Bob Henry's threatening to foreclose on the Retreat," she said, "You'll be out of work. And out of a home. You'll have to talk to him."

Daintree shrugged.

"I'd love to, but I'm afraid he won't listen to anything I say, these days".

"What have you done to him?" Valerie demanded.

"Not him," said Daintree, "his wife."

"And what have you done to her?"

Daintree placed her two hands together in a praying posture.

"I've led her on her pre-destined path to enlightenment; towards true emotional stability, creative expression and the pleasures of life."

Valerie turned to Rory.

"Do you understand a bloody word she's saying?" she asked.

Rory turned to Daintree.

"Could you explain in simple terms?" he asked. Then he added, "For Valerie's benefit." Although he too, had no idea what Daintree was talking about.

Daintree's little mouth pouted in exasperation.

Eventually she said, "Alright I'll explain it very simply. In a way the unenlightened will understand. Bob and his wife hadn't had sex for ten years."

"We gathered that much", said Valerie.

Daintree ignored her.

"I encouraged her to find her inner self. To lose her inhibitions, to express her true desires. To discuss her most secret fantasies with Bob."

"And?" said Valerie impatiently.

 Daintree shrugged, "None of her fantasies included him. In fact, they didn't include any man. Turns out all this time Bob's wife has been a latent homosexual. She's moved in with one of the other ladies on the course and is filing for divorce. Of course, this isn't a good time for Bob to have to give up half his worldly goods, but his wife is insisting on not a cent less. It looks like it'll end up in court. And it looks like he's taking it out on you."

If Bob foreclosed on Rory and Valerie they'd lose everything. But it was worse than that. The bank also had a mortgage on the Retreat. If Bob took the Retreat and the farmhouse, the bank would still want to be paid, or they would want the Retreat in lieu. Naturally Bob wouldn't give up the Retreat and it would all end up in court. Of course, Bob would win. The Trust actually owned the farm when Rory and Valerie used it as collateral to finance the Retreat. Still did. The bank would have to seek recompense from Rory and Valerie personally and no doubt there would be criminal charges for obtaining money under false pretences. Rory and Valerie could end up in jail.

Rory had always had an obsessive fear of going to goal. He was convinced that he would be sodomised there. It was a fear that had haunted him back in Sydney when he was being investigated for misuse of clients' money in the Stockbroking business.

It was a fear he'd expressed at the time to a notorious criminal with whom he was drinking, in an Eastern Suburbs pub. The criminal had been sitting on a high barstool at the time and he'd laughed so much that he'd fallen off the stool and lay on the bar-room floor, helpless with laughter.

"What's so funny?" Rory had asked, indignantly.

Still lying on the floor and laughing, the notorious criminal had pointed up at Rory's face.

"You?" he'd said, "You?... You're so bloody ugly. Nobody'd touch you with ten-foot pole."

Strangely, Rory didn't find this comforting. He was still convinced that if he ever went to jail, by the end of the first day he'd be wearing a flower behind one ear and keeping house for some enormous Bikie.

Now he was facing the prospect of prison again. There was only one thing to do: get in touch with Mike and try to do a deal with him. If the only two prospective heirs under the Will agreed that the Trust couldn't foreclose on Rory and Valerie, then it would seem unlikely that the courts would allow Bob to act against the wishes of all the potential future owners.

Unfortunately, Rory called when Mike wasn't in a very good mood; he was about to go into Cairns to have a blood test. This meant he was fasting and Mike was always very bad tempered when he was hungry. With nothing else to do, John was preparing to drive into town with him.

"And don't you go taking the blood test for him," Mary had warned John. "If Mike's blood test isn't very different from his last one and more like the one before, I'll be calling the police about a little incident in an abattoir."

Rory called Mike on Mike's mobile. It wasn't on speaker phone but Rory was talking so loudly in his effort to sound casual that everybody could hear him.

"Mike, m-a-a-te..." Rory said, "How are you, mate?"

Since moving to the country, Rory had acquired, and sometimes lost again, a broad Australian accent. In fact, he acquired a new accent just about everywhere he went.

He and Valerie had gone to New York for a month on their honeymoon and he'd returned to Australia sounding like Robert De Niro. Rory could assume or discard these accents at will and he hadn't been using his 'ocker' accent when Mike and Mary had visited them the last time, so Mike was a bit confused.

"Who is this?" he asked.

"It's Rory, mate," said Rory, "Your brother Rory. Hey mate, how about this bloody virus, eh? It's a bugger eh? You never know who's going to catch it. I was thinking, mate, in a time like this we could both drop off the twig. Wouldn't want our wives to be left penniless, would we? I was thinking, what do you say we make an agreement, no matter which one of us dies first, we share the Trust fifty-fifty?"

"Are you ill?" asked Mike, suspiciously.

"No, mate," said Rory, "Never fitter. I'm just thinking. Something like this makes you think, doesn't it? We gotta think of Mary and Valerie. Not to mention young Matthew and…"

He was going to mention Mike's grandson by name but he couldn't remember his name, so he said, "and his little one. What do you say? A fifty-fifty split? It's what you always wanted."

Mike held his phone away from his mouth.

"Rory wants an agreement to split the Trust fifty-fifty," he said to Mary.

He needn't have bothered. Mary had overheard everything and she was a lot sharper than Mike. A lot sharper and a lot better informed. While he was up on the Daintree fishing, she was watching the twenty-four-hour news. She knew what the virus was doing to business and it would only get worse. The Maguire Construction

Company would soon be grinding to a halt, laying people off. There wouldn't be buyers for many of the apartments they had already built or were in the process of building. The Company would be practically worthless. The only things in the Trust of value would be the macadamia farm, the farmhouse and the Retreat.

"Is the farmhouse and the Retreat included in the deal?" she asked Mike.

Mike passed the query on to Rory.

"Oh, no, mate," he said Rory. "Valerie 'n me have bought those. They're ours. I'm talking about the Trust."

Mary didn't need Mike to repeat the answer. She'd heard it.

"Tell him to fuck off," she said, or rather she yelled, so that Rory would be able to hear it and Mike wouldn't have to repeat it.

He repeated it anyway.

"Mary says fuck off," he said and hung up.

John had been listening in to all this, mesmerized. He wasn't entirely sure what was going on but he thought there might be a book in it. It wasn't likely he was going to find out, though.

"You can fuck off, too," Mary said, turning to him. "If they start putting us into isolation and closing borders, we could be stuck with you for months."

CHAPTER THIRTEEN

If Mary was rude to Rory and to John, at least she did it to their faces. In these days of social media that's a very old-fashioned thing to do. And very ineffectual. If you really want to insult somebody and destroy them, you do it anonymously... On-line.

As Valerie set out to do.

Not that she didn't give Mike fair warning. She phoned him, yelled abuse at him and warned him that if he didn't agree to a fifty/fifty split of the Trust with Rory and herself retaining the Retreat and the farmhouse, then he would be very sorry. She knew things about him, she said, things that would destroy him.

Mike had no secrets capable of destroying him; especially now that he had virtually isolated himself from the world and spent his time either on the property or up in the Daintree Rainforest fishing, so he ignored the threats. He assumed that there actually had to be secrets for Valerie to do him harm.

Rather naïve of him, really.

The first anonymous post was framed as a fond farewell but it was in fact a vicious blow.

"Congratulations to NSW Teacher Mike Maguire on his move to Far North Queensland. We're all very relieved but we hope this doesn't mean the Queensland Education Department are letting him teach young girls in Queensland schools."

Again, Mike underestimated the effect of this. He told Mary to ignore it when she pointed out the post to him.

He wasn't intending to return to teaching anyway.

The problem was, Mary had returned to teaching. On the day that Mike went to see the Cairns oncologist about his latest blood tests, Mary was called into the Principal's office at her new school and asked about her husband.

Mary explained that some years before, a girl had made a complaint against him, but that was all settled years ago. She was a troubled girl without a father. Mike had taken an interest in her; tried to help her. She had misinterpreted Mike's interest and when he made it clear that she was just a young girl and he was just a teacher looking out for the welfare of his students, she made a complaint against him.

"All lies, of course," said Mary. "There was an enquiry. There was nothing in it. The girl admitted as much later, but not until she'd also accused her psychiatrist of abusing her."

The Principal had no doubt that Mary believed that Mike had been wrongly accused. Her doubts lay in whether Mary was right to believe him. Women have a bad habit of only believing what they want to believe about their husbands; just as men have a bad habit of only believing what they want to believe about their wives. It wasn't a gender thing for the Principal. She was only concerned with the safety of the children and the school's reputation. She told Mary that she was sure Mary was telling the truth but, just to quell the gossip, Mike shouldn't come within two hundred metres of the school or attend any school functions.

Mary was furious, but it didn't bother Mike. He was happy to keep away from the school. He was much more worried about his first visit to the Cairns oncologist and the possibility of being put back on hormone therapy, chemotherapy or any other bloody therapy.

So, while the Oncologist sat, staring at his screen, comparing Mike's various blood tests, Mike decided to tell him the truth. Not the whole truth, of course, but enough of the truth for this oncologist to make a reasoned judgement.

"Your blood tests show some worrying variations," the Oncologist said after a period of silence.

"That's because the September test isn't mine," Mike answered. "There's been a mix-up. I didn't take a blood test in September." (Which was true, Mike told himself.) "They must be somebody else's results. Probably John Maguire's. The hospital often confused us. I'm sure we had each other's treatment at Radiology more than once."

The Oncologist found this hard to believe. Not that he was so naïve as to believe mistakes never happened. Seeing him hesitate, Mike pushed on.

"In any case the PSA reading isn't much higher than the earlier one, before September. Certainly, no reason to start the hormone treatment again, is it?"

"You're probably right," said the Oncologist, "I'm not that keen on hormone treatment after brachial and radiotherapy. If the cancer isn't cured, all it tends to do is hide the symptoms. But why don't we do another test anyway, just to be sure."

Mike was happy to do a new test. At least he was happy to take a new pathology request form from the Oncologist and head off for his main business of the day; which was buying a beehive and all the paraphernalia required to keep bees.

Mike had become interested in bees through his friendship with the indigenous Daintree Forest Ranger, Warren Hodgson. A lot of beekeepers took their beehives into the

Daintree Forest, Warren told him, where the rich variety of trees and flowers enabled the bees to produce a high quality honey, famous throughout the world. However, the Queensland Government had decreed that after 2024, all beehives would be banned from Queensland National Parks.

Warren was a bit ambivalent about this. He agreed that the National Parks should be preserved for nature rather than primary production, but his people had been harvesting honey from the Daintree for over twenty thousand years and he wasn't sure a few beehives did much environmental damage to the Rainforest. Although one thing he was sure of was that the move would cause a shortage of bees to pollinate the farmers' crops, and a shortage of honey. Already bee numbers had been depleted by the recent bush fires and loss of habitat. Without the National Parks, suitable places to keep bees would become even more rare.

All this peaked Mike's interest. He enjoyed fishing, but there was only so much time you could spend sitting in a boat. He hadn't wanted to go back to teaching, even before Valerie started her on-line campaign. But he was looking for something to do and in beekeeping, he thought he'd found an opportunity.

If habitat for bees was going to become scarce, then the bush around Mike's property, and the property itself, which was abundant with native species, would become very valuable as a bee keeping habitat.

"Even if," he'd joked to Mary, "the honey may have a tinge of marijuana to flavour it."

Mike had spoken to beekeepers tending their hives in the rainforest and to others with domestic set-ups. They seemed to fall into two categories: those who loved flow-hives, where you simply turned on a tap to harvest the honey; and those that believed flow-hives were unnatural and bad for the bees.

Warren was ambivalent about this, too. But essentially, he didn't think it mattered what type of hive you used. What was important, he said, was the skill of the bee-keeper rather than the design of the hive. So, Mike decided to buy one of each type of hive and see how they went, before deciding on which type he would use.

After seeing the oncologist, Mike visited a local bee-keeper where he bought a second-hand bee hive, a mask, a smoker and gloves. Then he visited a hardware store and bought a boiler suit and heavy wellington boots.

He was trying on his outfit when Mary arrived home from work. Despite her run-in with the Principal, the sight of Mike made her laugh. He looked like a front-line worker against Covid19, or maybe a visitor from outer space.

Mike didn't mind being the butt of Mary's jokes. He even felt that he sort-of deserved it. Their whole married life, Mike had been thinking up some scheme or other and never seeing it through. But this time, he assured Mary, it would be different. He had one beehive and had ordered a second one, a flow-hive from Northern New South Wales.

Mary didn't even know what a flow-hive was and over a long drink Mike explained to her the intricacies of flow-hives, normal hives and bee-keeping in general, with all the confidence of a man who had spent just half an hour researching the subject on the internet.

"Where are you going the get the bees from?" Mary asked.

"Catch them," said Mike, with surprising and totally misplaced confidence.

"How do you catch a hive of bees?" asked Mary, "One at a time?"

"No," said Mike, ignoring her raised eyebrows. "You find a swarm, looking for a new hive. Maybe they're hanging under a branch of a tree or the eaves of a house," he was quoting directly from the internet, "then you knock them down into a box, take the box to the empty hive and pour them in."

"Sounds tricky," said Mary.

"Yes," agreed Mike. "I could always buy a couple of swarms of bees, of course. But I'd rather catch them if I can."

Mary enjoyed listening to Mike talk; enjoyed the fact that he was enthusiastic about something again.

Although she was concerned when he mentioned that he'd bought a flow-hive from Northern New South Wales and he'd have to go and fetch it. There was talk that they were closing the New South Wales/ Queensland Border to stop the spread of the Covid19 Virus.

Mike wasn't worried. Beekeeping, he informed her, was considered to be primary produce, an essential industry. He was sure he would be able to drive through. They were letting Queensland residents through on business.

"You'll have to get your Queensland licence," Mary reminded him.

"On my list of things to do tomorrow," he said as he replenished their glasses.

"Is stopping Valerie from libelling you, on your list, too?" asked Mary. "The Principal spoke to me, today. They want you to stay at least two hundred metres away from the school."

"No worries," said Mike.

"Lots of worries," said Mary. "They're ruining your

reputation and mine. You've got to stop them, Mike."

"How?" asked Mike.

Mary had already thought about it.

"Do what you should have done last year," she said, "Tell the bank that Rory and Valerie took out a loan against property they didn't own."

"I can't do that," said Mike. "I'll phone Rory, tell him if the trolling doesn't stop immediately, I'll talk to the Bank. If we just go ahead and tell the Bank, he'll have no reason to stop trolling us. In fact, he'll have reason to go harder"

Mary could see the sense of this. They needed something to hang over Rory and Valerie's heads to make them stop. But she was worried Mike was just procrastinating.

"Well go on, then," she said.

"I'm just finishing my drink," Mike protested.

"Now," said Mary, in the voice she reserved for very naughty children.

Mike dialled the number.

It rang and rang.

"He's not answering, I'll try again later," he said, trying to put off the confrontation.

He was too late. Rory answered the phone.

"Mike," he said, "What can I do for you? Changed your mind about the Trust?"

Rory almost seemed to be laughing over the phone. In fact, he was slightly drunk but it sounded to Mike that he thought he had the upper hand. That, and the fact that Mary was watching intently and listening in, made Mike determined not to back down.

"No," he said, "But I have changed my mind about the bank. You're a thieving bastard and a bully, Rory. Always have been, even when we were kids. Well, no more. You either stop this trolling or I'm telling the bank you took out a mortgage on land you didn't own."

"Don't know what you're talking about, mate," said Rory, trying to bluff his way through. "Don't know about any... what did you call it, trolling?"

"Ask Valerie," said Mike, "Tell her that if it doesn't stop, I'm going to the bank. Not phoning them. Seeing them personally. I've got business in Northern New South Wales in the next few days. I'll be visiting them in person; so that there's no misunderstanding."

And he hung up.

"Bastard," he muttered under his breath.

Mary stood up and gave him a big hug.

"My hero," she said.

But at the other end things weren't quite so friendly.

"This is your bloody fault," Rory yelled at Valerie, "What did you have to get on the internet for?"

Valerie shrugged.

"I thought he'd give in. He always has before. It's not him, anyway, it's that bloody Mary. She's never liked us. Always been jealous."

"Jealous of what?" demanded Rory. "We're pushing sixty and we've got nothing. We're broke. We're in debt and we're facing bankruptcy and jail."

"You're pushing sixty," said Valerie, as if that was the worst thing he had said. "I'm nearly ten years younger than you."

"Four years," Rory reminded her. "Fat lot of good it'll do you anyway. Just means you'll live longer in jail. Just stop the trolling now."

"I can't" said Valerie. "It's not me anymore. All sorts of people have joined in. Probably people who have never even met him. People are crazy. Happy to rant at anybody.

I can't stop it."

"Jeez," said Rory, "I need a drink."

As if that would solve anything.

For the first time, the seriousness of their situation seemed to dawn on Valerie. She was immediately making plans.

"We could cash in everything and disappear overseas," she said.

"How?" yelled Rory. "They've cancelled all the planes because of the Covid virus. We can't even get into Queensland, let alone overseas. How the hell are we going to stop him going to the Bank?"

Valerie shrugged, despondently. "Even if we did, it still wouldn't help," she said, "We've still got the problem of Bob Henry and the other mortgage. The only way we can get out of this is if Mike dies suddenly.

"I could shoot him," said Rory. "He lives in the middle of nowhere, apparently. If Mary was at work, there would be no witnesses."

Rory didn't mean it, of course; it was just the drink talking. As it was when Valerie replied,

"Well, if you're going to shoot him, make sure you do it before he talks to the Bank Manager."

Initially neither of them meant it. But as they both sat there, getting more and more drunk, the idea seemed to get better and better. The border with Queensland was closing but there were hundreds of outback roads crossing the border. They couldn't all be manned by the police. Rory could use Google Earth on his computer to zoom in on those country roads, find one that didn't have a road block. Once in Queensland it would take a couple of days to get to where Mike and Mary lived. Rory could sleep in his Range Rover, wait for Mary to go to work, then move in.

Rory thought close range with a shotgun under the throat would look like suicide. He would use gloves, and then put the gloves on Mike to explain the lack of residue burns on his hands. He would be a few hundred miles south before Mary discovered Mike's body when she came home from school.

With everybody in social isolation because of the virus, nobody would even know Rory wasn't still at home. (Although they would have to cancel the cleaner, of course.)

They could even take a couple of pictures of themselves, in and around the Retreat; post them on the Retreat Website during the time Rory was away, proving he was still there the whole time.

The problem was Daintree. She was still in the Retreat. She'd know he wasn't there.

"Leave that to me," said Valerie.

And that was the last thing Rory remembered before he passed out.

CHAPTER FOURTEEN

The following morning Rory was woken by Valerie giving him a cup of tea, hot buttered toast, and a kiss. This hadn't happened since they were first married, well over a decade earlier. Rory wondered what he had done to deserve such treatment? Then he remembered.

He couldn't believe it. Surely Valerie hadn't taken the idea of murdering Mike seriously?

His hopes were soon dashed.

"I've spoken to Daintree," Valerie said, "She's agreed to give you an alibi."

Rory was stunned.

"You haven't told her I'm going to kill Mike?

"Of course not," said Valerie. "I wouldn't trust her with information like that."

Rory breathed a sigh of relief and was just about to take a sip of tea when Valerie added,

"I told her you were going to rob a bank."

Rory almost choked, spluttered, and spilt hot tea all down his bare chest and beyond, which led to him leaping about and yelling for a towel. Valerie fussed over him. She had to take good care of him; at least until he'd killed his brother.

It wasn't only Valerie who was now seeing Rory in a new light. Coming from the Gold Coast, Daintree was familiar with the criminal class. She found them rather exciting. Now she found Rory exciting. Well, perhaps not exciting, but more interesting.

Since she'd set herself up as a Healer, the two of them had drifted further and further apart. No more sneaking down to Daintree's quarters in the Retreat. Daintree's door was firmly locked at night. Rory had always been just a meal ticket to her and as she became more and more successful, the less she needed him.

Now with the virus closing down the Retreat, she needed him again. He was her meal ticket again. Besides, Valerie had offered her a third share of the Retreat. What Valerie hadn't pointed out was that Daintree would also owe a third of the mortgage on the Retreat and since the mortgage was actually higher than the Retreat's value, Daintree was getting nothing but a debt. No point in even mentioning that to Daintree, Valerie decided. Not when she was so impressed by the idea of Rory being an Armed Hold-up Man.

So impressed, in fact, that she brought him a gift; a crystal on a leather cord.

"A Carnelian crystal" she told him, "A nursing stone that helps stimulate initiative and dispel apathy and passivity. It's particularly useful in promoting the physical energy needed to take action in emotionally charged circumstances."

Rory had no idea what she was talking about but he accepted the gift and the kiss on the cheek as she draped it around his neck.

"When are you going on your 'little trip?'" she asked him; almost breathless with excitement.

"Oh, soon," said Rory, more and more convinced that he wasn't going to be able to get out of it. "It takes a lot of planning, you know?"

Daintree nodded.

"And you need to be in tip-top condition. Come down to

the Retreat and I'll put you through a yoga class. We can record it and put it on the Retreat's web page while you're away. It'll give you an alibi."

Rory liked the idea of another private yoga class with Daintree.

"Will it include Pelvic Rock Exercises?" he asked.

"Oh yes," she said, moving closer, "And a few other special movements that we won't video. Keep the Carnelian Crystal on, you'll need its energy."

He was just about to follow Daintree out when Valerie reappeared carrying a shotgun that looked like it was almost an antique.

"Found this in the farm shed," she announced, handing Rory the huge weapon. "Your dad used to use it to kill rats before we got the barn owls for the rainforest."

Rory took the gun reluctantly. He'd never liked guns. They made a lot of noise. Besides people could get hurt playing with guns.

Valerie watched him as he gingerly held the gun.

"You do know how to shoot a gun, don't you?" she asked.

Daintree was also watching. He couldn't admit that since he was a boy, he had always been frightened of firing guns.

"Course," he said. His voice dropping half an octave so that he sounded like his late father.

"Yeah, 'course," he repeated, "But this is a gun for shooting rats. For a bank robbery you need something more manageable. You need to cut the barrels off about here."

He prescribed a cut across the barrels of the shotgun almost down to the stock.

"Accuracy doesn't matter at close quarters. Manoeuvrability's everything," he explained, trying to prove he knew what he was talking about. Although he then spoilt the effect by putting the shotgun up to his shoulder and aiming at an imaginary target in the distance; something you never do with a sawn-off shot gun, which is fired from the hip.

"Boom, Boom," he said, quickly swinging the shotgun from one imaginary target to another.

Valerie and Daintree exchanged satisfied smiles. They'd found their hero... or was it their patsy?

If anything, Mary had even less faith in Mike than Valerie and Daintree had in Rory. While she was getting ready for school, he had found a cardboard packing box that they'd used in the move up to Queensland and he was cutting a circle out of one side, about eight centimetres in diameter. Then he stapled a piece of net over the hole to provide fresh air for the bees he hoped to catch in the box.

He put the lid back on the box and stood admiring his handiwork.

"That looks very dodgy to me," said Mary, "Wouldn't it be easier to just buy some bees?"

"No can do," said Mike. "This is the Covid19 age. People can't just go and buy anything they want. They have to find it for themselves. Hunter/Gatherers. The end of civilization as we know it. Besides, catching the bees yourself is half the fun."

"You do talk rubbish," said Mary, although things certainly had changed since the outbreak of the Covid19 virus in China just a few months earlier. People were afraid to send their kids to school. Attendances at Mary's school were down forty percent. The teachers were spending their time devising home learning packages in case schools closed completely and children had to be educated at home.

If Mary were honest, she was finding the whole challenge rather exciting. Rather than seeing Covid as the End of Civilisation, she saw it as a precursor to the future, when all education would be on-line and kids could learn anything they wanted from anybody they wanted, from anywhere in the world. Mary saw the Covid19 Virus as the future arriving early.

Not that she saw much future in Mike's beekeeping. Still, it kept him busy. As long as it didn't mean he didn't do all the things he needed to do, which included the shopping that had become harder and harder because people had started panic buying and the supermarkets were running out of essentials like toilet paper and rice.

"Make sure you go shopping. Oh, and get your Queensland driving licence," Mary said, as she gathered up her files and put them in her carry bag alongside her lap top.

"Okay, okay," said Mike, still pre-occupied with adding a few more staples to the box 'just in case.'

"Michael," Mary said, aware that he wasn't listening, "I mean it. Go shopping and get your new licence. If you don't, I'll come home and set fire to your bee box."

"Oh charming," said Mike, only half pretending to be hurt, "It wouldn't hurt if a bloke got some support around here."

"You're like a big kid," said Mary, kissing him on the cheek, "You're worse than my Grade Ones."

"Am not," said Mike, sounding just like a Grade One, but Mary was already out the door and Mike soon forgot about it. He had to collect some dry leaves to see if his bee-smoker worked.

Rory was also procrastinating. It wasn't that he didn't want his brother dead. He had fantasied about that ever since he first learnt the terms of his father's Will; which, he assumed was his father's intention when he wrote the Will. Mostly he dreamt of some unforeseen disaster befalling Mike: a road accident, an attack by a wild dog perhaps. Subconsciously he had only bought the mutt that now paced up and down the enclosure near the house, because he knew Mike was afraid of dogs. Although he hadn't seemed too afraid when he'd hurled abuse at the dog and woke everybody up the last time he and Mary had come to stay; the time he had left in the middle of the night after writing to Bob Henry telling him they had borrowed money against the farm.

That alone was reason enough to kill Mike. It was none of Mike's business. As Mary had said at the time, it didn't affect him. The only thing that affected anything was who died first, and Rory was determined that it would be Mike, even if it meant Rory would have to kill him.

The problem was Rory was scared. He wondered if there was some third-hand, long-distance way he could kill Mike. Maybe get hold of some Covid-19 Virus and post it to him. But knowing Rory's luck, he would probably contact the disease himself, posting the virus, and Mike would probably survive, or the virus would get stuck in the post and die before it reached Mike.

Rory tried to think of some more practical alternatives. He thought about poison; about arranging an accident. Nothing seemed to work. In the end, he concluded that Valerie was right. The only option was to shoot him and make it look like suicide.

Rory had seen CSI shows on television. He knew about blood splatter patterns and gunshot residue on the hands of anybody who had fired a gun. He considered wearing gloves, then taking the gloves off afterwards and putting then on Mike's hands so that the gunshot residue would be there. But what if they checked the inside of the gloves for DNA and found his DNA?

Maybe he should keep the gloves and dispose of them later? But then, what if they tested Mike's hands and found no gunshot residue? Rory sat up in bed most of the night, trying to think it through.

Eventually Valerie switched on the bedside light and sat up beside him in bed.

"You're over complicating it," she said, "Mike lives in Far North Queensland. There's hardly likely to be a genius pathologist or detective up there. They'll see a shotgun and a dead body and they'll say suicide. Especially after all the terrible things people have been saying about Mike on social media."

"People?" queried Rory. "It was you."

"So?" said Valerie, "I've given him a motive. What more do you want? Course, if you're scared, if you want to go to jail…"

"I'm not scared," said Rory, trying to keep the tremor out of his voice.

"It's settled, then," said Valerie, and she turned out the light, lay down, turned her back on Rory and went back to sleep, while Rory sat up, still worrying.

Eventually he must have dozed off, but he woke up screaming.

He had been dreaming. He had dreamt that he'd blown Mike's head off but that Mike hadn't died. Rory had turned away from the bloody mess, only to have Mike grab his arm, swing him around, and demand through a face that was now just a bloody hole, what Rory thought he was doing.

Mike grabbing his arm in the dream coincided exactly

with Valerie grabbing his arm to wake him up. Rory always wondered how that happened. How events in his dreams coincided exactly with events in his life? The dream must have known that Valerie was about to shake him, or the dream was instantaneous and happened at the moment Valerie grabbed him.

"How could that be?" he wondered. The dream seemed to go on for ages.

It wasn't a mystery he was going to solve because there was nobody that he could discuss it with. Valerie certainly wasn't interested.

"I'm going to Lismore," she said, "I'll buy you a sleeping bag, some food and a portable camping stove. You can't stay in hotels or eat in restaurants on your way up. Nobody must know you're in Queensland. Is there anything else you want while I'm out?"

Rory wanted another plan, but he wasn't going to tell Valerie that. So, he shook his head, got out of bed and shuffled to the bathroom, feeling quite groggy from the lack of sleep.

After a good breakfast, Rory felt better. Instead of feeling, tired, frightened and hungry, he now only felt tired and frightened. But he staggered down to the farm work shed with the shotgun and went looking for a hacksaw and a bench vice.

It was still a couple of months before the macadamia harvest was due and Rory had taken advantage of the lull to lay off his farm manager until such time as the harvest started. There was a danger, of course, that when the harvest did start the farm manager wouldn't want to return or had found work elsewhere. But with so many people out of work with the Covid Virus Rory doubted he would have any trouble finding somebody else. Besides he had a rudimentary knowledge of harvesting himself. If needs must, he could drive the harvester, put the nuts into the dehusker, float them to show they were fully mature, dry them in the silos for a few days, and ship them off to the processor. That's what he told himself, anyway.

He clamped the shotgun into the vice, and stood there, wondering where one should make the cut in the barrel of a shotgun. Should he cut it off right next to the stock or should he leave a length of barrel still attached? He was still staring down at the gun, his head in a complete haze when Daintree walked into the shed.

Although it wasn't Daintree, it was Roxette.

She had abandoned her flowing robes and crystals. Her hair was now tied back in a tight pony tail. She wore a man's shirt and jeans, a leather belt and R. M. Williams boots.

"G'day," she said, adopting the patois of the criminal class, "What yuh doing?"

Rory stared at her in surprise. Obviously, she had undergone another metamorphosis. She had gone from Meter Maid to Aspiring Actress to New Age Guru. Now she was going from New Age Guru to Gangster's Moll; her Bonnie to his Clyde.

Roxette didn't wait for Rory to reply. She could see what he was doing, or rather not doing.

"Cuttin' down the shotgun, eh? Mind if I do it?"

"Do you know how to do it?"

"Course," said Roxette, "I did metalwork at school."

She started rummaging around in the toolbox on the bench and dug out a set-square and a marking pencil. She put the setsquare alongside the barrel of the shot-gun and drew a line across both barrels an inch or so from the stock. She checked the line was square, flicking away any imaginary dust around the line as she did so. Then she picked up the hacksaw and started cutting along the line.

"How come you did metalwork?" Rory asked.

"That's where the boys were, wasn't it?" asked Roxette, rhetorically, "Only girls did Home Economics. Well, girls and a couple of poofs."

Roxette continued sawing off the first barrel of the shotgun. The screeching noise set Rory's teeth on edge but he said nothing. He just stood there, gritting his teeth.

He wasn't sure he liked the new Roxette.

In fact, he was sure he didn't like her but he wasn't going to stop her from helping him. She really did know what she was doing with the hacksaw. She used long smooth strokes of the saw and kept the cut mark exactly on the drawn line. Before she finished cutting off the first barrel, she had tilted the hacksaw so that it started cutting into the second barrel as well. That way she made sure the two barrels were cut off exactly parallel and the same distance from the stock. Then she set aside the hacksaw and carefully filed the rough sawn-off edges of the barrels until that they were smooth and even.

She took the gun out of the vice, brushed any loose filings away with her hand, blew on both barrels to make sure they were clean, and inspected her handiwork.

It was a pretty good job, even if she said so herself. Certainly, better than Rory would have done.

"Let's give 'er a go," she said, "You got any cartridges?"

"Up at the house," said Rory.

"Well let's go, then" said Roxette, and she led the way, still clinging to the shotgun.

They went deep into the rainforest to test the gun. Roxette took two cartridges from Rory and loaded both barrels. She selected a large fig tree with its wide expanse of roots, as a target not even Rory could miss, but she didn't hand him the shotgun. Instead, she fired from about six feet away, holding the shot gun at waist level just like she'd seen in the movies, straight into the tangle of roots.

Rory closed his eyes and jumped nervously. When Roxette discharged the second barrel, he jumped again, even though he knew what to expect. Roxette ejected the spent cartridges from the shot-gun, and went forward to check her handiwork. Even from just six feet away the shotgun blast spread out across almost six feet of tree trunk and root system but the pellets were still deeply embedded in the wood.

"That should do the trick, "Roxette nodded. "From a couple of meters, you'll practically cut someone in half... You wanna try?"

"Better not," said Rory. "Too much shooting might attract attention."

"Not down here," said Roxette, "We're miles from anywhere."

But she didn't push it. She suspected, correctly, that Rory was afraid of guns. Which, she thought, could be a problem in an armed holdup.

"Can I come?" she asked.

"Come where?"

"On the robbery. I could drive the getaway car; get a back-up gun."

"It's not going to be that sort of a robbery," said Rory, thinking quickly "I'm going to kidnap a bank manager, get him to open the bank safe outside of working hours, then I'll tie him up and slip away."

"He might put up a struggle," said Roxette.

"He won't," snapped Rory, at last positive about something. How could he struggle? He didn't exist.

Immediately he regretted snapping at Roxette. It was just his nerves but he couldn't tell her that. Anyway, he didn't need to tell her. She already knew. Even when Rory added, in a more conciliatory voice,

"I'll need you here to release the yoga videos and give me an alibi."

Roxette didn't push it. Nor did she object when Rory took the shotgun and said he was going up to the farmhouse to take a nap. She let him go but she collected her car from the Retreat and drove it up to where she could watch both the farmhouse and the farm gate.

As soon as Valerie returned from her shopping, Roxette drove up to the farmhouse and parked behind her.

"Give you a hand?" she called to Valerie.

"Thanks," said Valerie, "I'll just get the keys to Rory's Range Rover."

"Use my car," Roxette said, "It's got Queensland number plates. If the cops see Rory driving around with New South Wales number plates, they might stop him."

"Good idea," said Valerie, and without consulting Rory, since neither of them had much confidence in him anyway, Valerie started packing supplies into the back of Roxette's Subaru Legend.

It was true that Rory was less likely to be stopped by the police in Queensland if he were driving a car with Queensland number plates, but that wasn't the reason Roxette had suggested that he use her car. When she bought the car, or rather when Rory bought the car for her, they had an anti-theft location device installed that meant she could locate her car at any time, using her mobile phone.

Watching Rory earlier, she was convinced he wouldn't have the nerve to carry out what she thought was an armed robbery. She intended to follow him when he went north, using the tracking device. She really wanted the robbery to take place. She really wanted a share of the Retreat. More than that she really wanted to be involved in the crime, and to get her own gun, but having observed Rory at close quarters, she wasn't at all sure Rory was in any fit state to go through with it.

"Did Rory sleep last night?" she asked Valerie.

"Not till almost dawn," said Valerie. "I told him he's over complicating it. How hard can it be?"

"I dunno," said Roxette, still retaining her gangster's moll persona. "It's not easy kidnapping somebody on your own."

Valerie had no idea what Roxette was talking about.

"Kidnapping?" she asked.

"The bank manager," said Roxette.

"Oh, yes," said Valerie, "Well, he's got a sawn-off shotgun. Not many people are going to argue with a sawn-off shotgun."

Roxette didn't disagree. But she knew that it wasn't just the shotgun that frightened people; it was the conviction of the person holding the gun. And Roxette had no confidence that Rory would be anywhere near threatening enough. She needed to be there to make sure nothing went wrong. Even then she needed Rory to be in tip top condition; not the nervous wreck he'd been that morning.

"He needs a proper sleep," she said, "I'll give him a massage with essential oils tonight. Lavender and jasmine."

"Do you really think that'll make him sleep?" asked Valerie.

"Yeah," said Roxette, "'specially if we put a couple of

sleeping tablets in his scotch. Knock him out while we prepare everything. Then when he wakes up, we get him out of here, on the road before he has time to think about it."

CHAPTER FIFTEEN

Dinner that evening had a decidedly surreal feeling for Rory. He was about to kill a man. Not just any man: his own brother. And there were Roxette and Valerie chatting away, as if this was the most normal thing in the world; discussing the best route to take over the Queensland border to avoid a police block and what Rory should tell the police if they did stop him.

"Tell them you're going to visit your brother in Far North Queensland," said Valerie, "Tell them he's got cancer."

Rory was sceptical.

"Do you think I should mention my brother?" he asked.

"Course," said Roxette, really getting into the spirit of the thing, "Tell them with all this self-isolation, you're worried that he might kill himself. They reckon people get depressed being locked up alone."

Rory looked suspiciously at Valerie. Had she told Roxette what was really going on?

But Valerie was looking equally suspiciously at him.

Rory decided that Valerie had said nothing. Roxette was just repeating chatter from television Expert Psychologists who were constantly harping on about the adverse effects of isolation since the pandemic had started.

Still, Rory doubted isolation would be depressing Mike.

"He isn't alone." he said, assuming Roxette knew nothing, "His wife's with him."

"But she's at work all day, isn't she?" said Valerie, sensing that Rory was looking for a way out of killing his brother. She turned to Roxette to explain. "She's a teacher."

"There you are then," said Roxette, "She's at work all day, being useful. He's stuck at home, useless, dying anyway. No wonder he's suicidal."

Roxette sounded so sincere that it shocked Rory. It shocked him even more when she burst out laughing.

"You know, I'm good at this," she said, "I should come along with you; I'd have the cops in tears, and giving us a police escort."

"That's the last thing we need," said Valerie, "Rory's going alone. Besides we need you to put on the videos to show he's still here."

"Yeah, sure," said Roxette, "Only joking," and she refilled everyone's wine glasses.

She didn't want to share the fact that she would be following Rory north, not even with Valerie.

"Bottoms up," she said, and Rory drained his glass in one go and pushed it forward for a refill.

This time Valerie didn't complain about Rory's drinking, as she usually did. Instead she and Roxette chatted on as if they were the best of friends, even though Rory knew they hated each other. Then again, maybe they didn't. Maybe Valerie liked this new incarnation of Roxette. Rory just found it bloody confusing. When he'd first met Roxette, she'd been a naïve little Meter Maid in a gold lame bikini, then she'd morphed into a Gold-Digger who managed to persuade Rory to pay her rent as well her acting lessons, dance lessons, and even a complete make-over. Rory knew everything was designed to get her big break at the Warner Brother Studios after which, Rory also knew, she'd dump him. Then she'd morphed again into a New Age Healer and Shaman, and now she'd become a

Gangster's Moll, practically salivating at the prospect of committing a robbery and maybe shooting someone.

Rory just didn't understand her. He had no idea who the real Roxette was. And as for Valerie, the most misogynistic woman he knew, sitting there as if she and Roxette were the greatest of friends; Rory didn't know her either.

Mind you, that was nothing unusual. He'd been married to Valerie for over ten years and he'd never understood her. Never understood why he'd married her. Obviously, all she was after was his money. Yet she'd stuck by him when he'd run afoul of the law with his stockbroking business. Probably playing the long game, Rory decided; waiting for Mike to die so Rory would inherit his father's Trust. Well, now the time had come. Maybe when he did get hold of the Trust, he could get rid of Valerie, too. Pay her off. Pay Roxette off. Go away somewhere. Start again. Maybe in the tropics, like his brother. But of course, his brother wouldn't be there. He'd be dead.

The thoughts swirled in his head.

He was vaguely aware of Roxette telling Valerie that she'd changed her password on her computer to Bonnie, as in 'Bonnie and Clyde.'

They'd laughed.

That was the last thing he heard.

His mind swirled and swayed, then went black, and he fell forward. His head banged on the table, but he didn't feel it. He had already passed out.

Valerie used her thumb to prise open one of his eyes. It stared unseeingly into the middle distance. Valerie let his eyelid clamp shut again.

"You don't think you've overdone it, do you?" she asked, not overly concerned.

"No," said Roxette, who had slipped more than one Mickey Finn to middle-aged businessmen visiting the Gold Coast.

On those occasions she'd borrowed their credit cards to make a few purchases while they slept, so she had to know how long they'd be unconscious. She had invariably used the touch and pay option on the credit cards. The only problem with it was the one hundred dollar limit, but even that had its advantages. No self-respecting married businessman was going to the police over a couple of one hundred dollar purchases, especially when she spent the money in ordinary places like super-markets, liquor stores and clothes stores. And Roxette always left their cash in their wallets and returned their credit cards, so they had no idea they'd been robbed until they were back home in Sydney or Melbourne, or maybe overseas. Even then they probably couldn't remember whether they'd made the purchases themselves, or not.

"The amount of drugs and alcohol he's had," Roxette told Valerie, authoritatively, "He'll get a good twelve hours sleep. Long enough to sleep off most of the hang-over. We should have him on the road by midday tomor-row. Come on, let's get him to bed."

As they carried him to the master bedroom and Roxette expertly undressed him and rolled him over onto his back, so that he was comfortable and wouldn't wake up with a sore neck or any other aches and pains, Val-erie wondered if Roxette had ever drugged her husband before.

She certainly seemed to be expert at it. And there she was, passing herself off as a Psychic New Age Healer. She was just a con-woman. She really had missed her voca-tion; she was obviously a great actress. She'd fooled Rory.

She'd fooled Bob Henry. She'd even fooled Valerie for a while.

But Valerie was something of an actor herself.

She helped Roxette put Rory to bed and even offered her another drink, but Roxette declined. She needed her beauty sleep, she said, and headed off for the Retreat down in the rainforest, saying she'd be back in the morning to get Rory on his way.

Valerie watched her go, then she switched off all the lights; but she didn't go to bed, not even in the guest bedroom. She went into the home office and logged into the Retreat's business computer using Roxette's password, "*Bonnie*."

Roxette had a motive for giving Valerie her password; but Valerie, who knew nothing of Roxette's plans had her own reason for using the password to log in to Roxette's account. Up to this point, she had conducted her social media trolling against Mike using public computers from the local library. Now with the Covid19 lockdown in place the library was closed. Obviously, Valerie couldn't use her own password in case the trolls were traced back to her, but she felt the trolling needed a little more tweaking if Mike's suicide was going to be accepted without question.

She realised that, so far, the trolling probably hadn't bothered Mike that much. He had retired anyway. He didn't care what people thought of him. But he did care what people thought about Mary. He did care about her career. And this was the element Valerie intended to add: a new troll from a young student of Mike's - Valerie would call her '*Roxette*' - who had been lured to his home under pretence of tutoring and had been abused. And the worst thing, '*Roxette*' added in her troll, was that at the time of the abuse, Mike's wife, who was also a teacher, was in the house. Valerie didn't actually claim that Mary was involved in the abuse, just left the hint that she knew about it. Not enough to start an enquiry against Mary. Just enough to sow the seeds of doubt.

Mary was oblivious to all this when she headed off to work early the following morning. It was to be a pupil-free day, giving the staff the opportunity to discuss a revised schedule for Covid-safe teaching. To her surprise, Mike was up before her. He had cooked her breakfast and as she ate, he was assembling his beekeeper's outfit of boiler suit, wellington boots, hat and gloves, together with the bee box and bee smoker, and was preparing to head off into the nearby bush.

The previous evening when he had been checking on his marijuana crop and harvesting a few leaves and seeds 'for medicinal purpose only', he had become aware of several bees, buzzing around the edge of the marijuana plantation.

Because he only harvested small amounts of marijuana for his and Mary's use, and the occasional smoke with Warren up in the Daintree, the plantation had grown far bigger than he had intended and it took some time to follow the bees through the plantation and into the nearby rainforest. He thought there must be a nest nearby where he might be able to harvest the Queen, so that the rest of the bees would follow her back to his first beehive in the clearing, not far from the house.

The buzzing had become louder, but he couldn't actually see any bees.

Then he saw it.

Better than a bees' nest, a swarm of bees, sheltering under an overhanging branch about three metres up in a yellow cedar tree. A swarm looking to build a nest, or to inhabit a beehive.

Perfect. All Mike had to do was persuade the swarm into his bee box and introduce them to his beehive.

"It sounds dangerous to me," Mary said when he told her his plan. "Don't you think you should get help?"

"From who?" Mike asked.

"How about Warren?" she suggested.

Warren was up in the Daintree Forest. Mike didn't feel he could impose on him to travel all the way down to the house. Didn't feel he needed to.

"It's a two-hour drive to the Daintree. Four hours for the round trip. I can have the bees in the hive hours before he's even half way here. Besides, it's a swarm, looking for a place to build a nest. If they don't find something, they could move on. They could be gone by the time Warren got here."

"Well, wait until I've finished work" Mary said, "and I'll help you."

"You don't know anything about capturing a swarm of bees," he said.

"Neither do you," she replied.

"Yes, I do. I've looked it up on the internet. Talked to people. You just put your box under the swarm, and you bang the branch they're hiding under. Then the bees just fall into the box. Well, not all of them, but as long as the Queen bee falls into the box, the rest of the swarm will follow her. Then you just put the lid on, and bob's your uncle."

"I'm sure it isn't that easy," said Mary. "Besides you know I don't like you climbing up ladders at your age. Not when you're on your own"

"The swarm's only a couple of metres off the ground," Mike lied, "I doubt I'll even need a ladder."

"Well, all right, then," said Mary, "But if you do need a ladder, just wait until I get back. I'm hoping to persuade the principal that we can do on-line lessons from home from now on, so I should be back soon."

"Yeah, sure," he lied again; and he walked her out to her car, kissed her goodbye, and watched her drive away. Then he gathered up his beekeeping equipment and collected the extension ladder from the garage.

As he pulled the ladder from its hooks on the wall, it caught on other tools hanging nearby; a chainsaw and a wicked looking scythe that he had used when they first bought the house and the grass was far too tall to mow. The tools fell to the ground. Mike thought about picking them up and then decided he wouldn't bother. He'd handle it when he got back from collecting the swarm of bees.

The first person that Mary bumped into at school was Deidre, her teacher's aide. Deidre was one of the first friends Mary had made at the school, so it was with no great pleasure that she greeted Mary with, "Have you seen the latest troll?"

"I don't look at them anymore," said Mary, "Mike doesn't seem bothered."

"This isn't about Mike. It's about you."

"Me?"

"Somebody called Roxette Simpson claims she was abused by your husband."

Mary shook her head, shocked.

"Never heard of her."

"She reckons she visited him at your home in Sydney. She says you were there."

"That's ridiculous," Mary said, "I'm really going to have speak to Mike. Get him to get off his arse and get in touch with the police. And get in touch with the bank about his brother."

"What's his brother got to do with it?" Deidre asked.

"Everything," said Mary, tight-lipped. "Him and his viperish wife. They're behind all this."

Mary wasn't able to explain further because they had arrived at the staff room where the seating was arranged with the regulation one-and-a-half metres distance between each person. Nobody shook hands. Nobody touched. Because of the virus. But Mary felt, sensed really, that not all the distancing she was getting was due to the virus.

She thought that perhaps she was being overly sensitive but her worst fears were confirmed when it came to discussing on-line teaching for kids who didn't need to come to school or had parents in vital jobs who were unable to look after them all day. With systems like Zoom and Skype, teachers could have the whole class up on screen together and hold proper lessons. Mary's point was that if the kids were at home, why couldn't the teachers be at home, too? In Mary's case it would have the advantage of also giving the kids natural history lessons about her garden; Mike's beekeeping, for example.

Mary had barely mentioned Mike's name when the Principal cut in.

"There will be no internet connection between teachers and pupils except through the school, on school computers," she said. "And each class will be supervised."

The other teachers nodded in agreement.

"Can't have the kids online unsupervised," said one of the teachers whom Mary had never liked, "Much too open to abuse."

Nobody mentioned the trolling. Nobody mentioned Mike. But Mary knew.

If she could have got hold of Valerie at that moment, she would have happily throttled her. Still, revenge is a dish best served cold, Mary told herself. As soon as the meeting was over, she would head home and insist Mike call Rory's Bank Manager. Then they'd call the Police. Then they'd call Bob Henry the Executor of the Family Trust, the Local Newspapers, the Northern New South Wales Newspapers, the TV Stations and the Radio Stations. Valerie had no idea what a torrent she had unleashed.

Blissfully unaware of his wife's predicament, Mike set out for the rainforest to locate the swarm of bees again. They weren't hard to find, but it was a lot harder than he'd expected, getting all his equipment into the forest. The boiler suit and wellington boots were hot and cumbersome. The gloves were so thick that he found it hard to carry things, and in the end he had to make a couple of trips into the rainforest and back. Eventually he had all his equipment in a neat pile on the ground next to the tree where the bees were swarming. He leaned his ladder against the branch where the swarm was buzzing away. Then he climbed the ladder wearing his protective gloves and hat and carrying the bee smoker, the bee box and a heavy stick to beat the tree.

He could carry them all up, but once he'd got there, he was helpless. The gloves made it impossible to hold the bee box with one hand under the swarm, while he sprayed smoke on them to calm them down with the other and then beat the overhead branch with the stick, all the time managing to hang on to the ladder with his knees.

His first attempt almost had him falling and he had to hang on to the ladder and branch for grim death, causing him to drop the stick, the smoker and the bee box.

Eventually he climbed back down the ladder and removed his gloves. Then he was able to pick up the box and the stick but the smoker would have to stay where it was on the floor.

He gingerly climbed the ladder again, held the box under the swarm, then, gripping the ladder with his knees, he repeatedly hit down on the branch.

At the third blow, the swarm detached from the branch. Most of the bees, including the Queen fell dutifully into the box but other bees started angrily buzzing around him. Mike didn't know if they were small worker bees or the larger drones which have no stingers; but he soon found out.

He was stung several times on the hands. It hurt so much he dropped the box onto the ground. His first thought was not to lose the bees; he slid down the ladder, ignoring the excruciating pain in his hands. He picked up the box lid and stuck into onto the box. Not all the bees were inside the box but most of them were. That would just have to do. He took off his helmet and inspected his hands. They were grotesquely swollen.

He knew, because he'd read it on the internet, that it took a thousand bee stings to kill a man. He had maybe half a dozen stings, but he still felt hot and short of breath. He needed help fast. He scrambled to get his phone out of his pocket, which was in his trousers, underneath the boiler suit.

He was stung again on the face.

He slapped at his face to remove the bee. The pain in his hand was agonising.

Eventually he pulled out his phone but it got caught in his boiler suit and with swollen hands he dropped it. He dropped to his knees to pick it up but he couldn't get a grip on it. His breath became even shorter.

It felt like his throat had swollen and closed up completely. He pitched forward, panting.

He should have studied the internet more carefully. It does take a thousand bees to kill an average adult man. But if the man were allergic to bee stings, it would only take one.

And for the first time, Mike realized that he was allergic to bee stings.

CHAPTER SIXTEEN

Mary had grown more and more angry as she drove home. Her mood didn't improve when she could find no trace of Mike at the house.

Eventually she set off, following the drag marks of the ladder into the rainforest, all the time yelling at him,

"Mike, where the bloody hell are you?"

And then she saw him, lying face down on the ground, the bee box beside him and bees still buzzing around, trying to get into the box to join their Queen.

Mary let out a shriek,

"Mike!"

She rushed forward; knelt beside him.

As if they knew better, the bees stayed clear of her. None of them tried to sting her. They wouldn't dare. She gently rolled Mike onto his back. His lips looked like the rubber tires from his golf buggy. His hands were bulbous masses.

Suddenly, Mike's phone rang. Instinctively she answered it.

"Hello?"

"Mrs. Maguire?" said a friendly voice, "This is Martin Woods from Free-Flow Hives. Your hive is ready. Are you going to pick it up or should we deliver?"

"Fuck your Free-Flow Hive," said Mary, and hung up.

She needed to call for help. But what was the point? Mike was dead. Nobody could help him now. Rory and

Valerie had won. No point in calling the bank. Rory owned the farm and the Retreat now. They owned the Trust now. They'd beaten Mike. Poor Mike. He would so hate that.

But she could still call the police? Accuse Rory and Valerie of trolling. Still go to the media. Get those bastards for blackening Mike's name... and hers.

But was it a story? Mike had been killed by his bloody bees. No evidence that Rory and Valerie were to blame. No evidence that they had ruined his life. He was happily keeping bees when he died. She still had her job. Nobody would care.

Mike being dead changed everything.

Then it struck her.

Nobody knew Mike was dead. If she could keep it a secret, just long enough to talk to the Bank Manager, report the trolling, go the police, go to the media.

But then what? She'd have to produce a week-old, or even two-week-old corpse. That would be the news -story then. Everybody would think she was a crazy woman, driven mad by grief and revenge. Rory and Valerie might get a bit of bad publicity, but they'd survive. Have a good laugh about it, while Mike went to his grave, his reputation in ruins. She couldn't just hang on to a dead body for a few weeks: or could she?

Mike had obviously died from bee stings. No foul play. No suspicious circumstances. If she could hide the exact time of his death, she would be in the clear.

She could move the beehives up into the Daintree Forest. She could move Mike's body up there and leave it by the hive... No, leave it by the hives, plural, because she would need to collect the free-flow hive and take both hives up to the Daintree. Obviously if he was found next to the free-flow hive, he must have died after it was delivered.

But what about decomposition? Surely, they'd know how long he'd been dead. And where would she hide him until it was safe for him to be found?

Then she realized that the answer to both questions were one and the same.

She had a freezer in the garage, big enough to hide several bodies, if need be. If she kept him there, still in his beekeeping gear, he would keep for weeks. When she took him up to the Daintree he would thaw out and look like a brand-new corpse. Always supposing, of course, that he wasn't found before he was thawed out, but with the Covid virus, tourists weren't allowed in the Daintree. It wasn't likely anybody would find him.

She knelt alongside her husband for a long time. Could she do this? Was it disrespectful to Mike? Neither of them was religious. She wasn't worried about his immortal soul, or hers, for that matter. She was worried about his memory, his legacy. She couldn't let him go to his grave as a reputed child molester. She couldn't let Rory and Valerie destroy his memory as well as steal his money.

Well, that was the theory. What about the practice? How the hell was she going to get Mike's body into the freezer? Then she remembered the hand-operated forklift that Mike used... used to use... to put his boat onto the campervan.

It was surprisingly easy to get Mike's body into the freezer. Mary put the two oars from the boat onto the forks of the forklift, then, with the forks at ground level, she rolled Mike's body onto the oars, which kept him rigid, even though rigor mortis hadn't yet set in.

Then she wheeled him into the garage, raised the forklift level with the top of the freezer and rolled him off the oars, into the freezer. He had been face-down as she'd carried him on the forklift, so that, as she rolled him over, he landed on his back in the freezer and stared up at her. Actually, he didn't stare up at her. His face was so swollen he looked like he had gone fifteen rounds with Mike Tyson. His lips were puffed up. His eyes were forced shut by the swelling around them.

Mary closed the freezer door, sat down on the fork-lift, and had a good cry.

Eventually she pulled herself together. She told herself she didn't have much time. She needed to move fast before somebody discovered Mike's body or realized he was missing.

She went back to the site of the accident and collected the bee box, Mike's gloves and hat, the smoker and his phone. Then she looked up recent calls and rang Martin Woods back.

"Sorry about the rudeness earlier," she said, "My husband and I were having a little trouble. Don't bother to send the hive, we'll come and collect it in the next couple of days."

Her plan was to go down to Northern New South Wales, pick up the beehive, visit the Bank and the police. Then she realized she would need help.

She wasn't a beneficiary of the will. She needed Mike to talk to the Bank Manager, but Mike was dead. Could she send an email? Would it be acknowledged? How do you forge a digital signature?

Maybe she should call her son, Matthew. He was a whiz at computers. On the other hand, he was painfully honest. Could he pretend his father was still alive? Could

Mary ask him to do it? She would have to tell him Mike was dead. She dreaded the thought. Matthew wasn't that close to his father but he loved him, and little Lucas would be devastated. Better to keep them in the dark until she had cleared Mike's name.

What she needed was somebody who was prepared to bend the law when it suited them.

Then a thought occurred to her.

She went through the list of contacts on Mike's phone and called John Maguire.

"Gooday, Mike," said John, expecting a call from his benefactor.

"It isn't Mike," said Mary, "He can't come to the phone at the moment but he wants you to do him a favour. He wants you to pick up a beehive for him."

"Oh? Where is it?" asked John.

"In Lismore," said Mary.

"I don't know," said John, "You know, with these travel restrictions in place..."

"It isn't that hard to travel around, as long as you stay in the state," said Mary, "I'll meet you in Lismore. You can help me load the beehive into the campervan."

"Can't you get them to post it?" asked John.

Mary just changed the subject.

"Did you hear the man who got trampled at the abattoir is never going to walk again?" she asked, "Be a real shame if they found out who was responsible."

"Are you blackmailing me?" John sounded shocked.

"Yes," said Mary.

And she hung up.

CHAPTER SEVENTEEN

Mary had already loaded up the campervan and set off to drive down to Lismore when Rory, still down on the farm, eventually rose from his drug-induced slumber.

She had also made other preparations. She had booked an appointment with Rory's bank manager and checked with Mike's old school to find out if there ever was a student there called Roxette Simpson. Of course, there wasn't; and the school, despite the heavy workload imposed on them by the Covid19 restrictions, promised to dig out and email Mary the report of the investigation into the original complaint by the schoolgirl, as well as the subsequent investigation of her allegations against her psychologist.

And Mary had also packed Mike's New South Wales driving licence, his credit cards, his razor, a pair of scissors and his beard trimmer, as well as a set of his clothes; the ubiquitous khaki shorts and shirt and RM Williams boots.

Roxette had been busy too. She'd bought a gun, explaining that, with the farm being unattended due to the virus, rats and feral cats were running wild in the rainforest and macadamia plantation. Then she bought a pair of stockings and some 'uppers' from the local drug dealer in Byron Bay, who was still working despite the lockdown. In fact, he was busier than ever, he said, doing home deliveries.

She bought enough food and water to last the several

days she expected that she would be away, following Rory. She packed everything into Rory's Range Rover and waited for him to wake up.

When he did awake, she gave him one of the uppers, saying it was paracetamol for his hangover, fed him a late breakfast and hurried him on his way, before he had a chance to change his mind.

Valerie took a back seat in all this. Roxette seemed to have far greater control over Rory than she did; she was better off just keeping out of the way. In fact, she hardly spoke until Rory was on the road, in Roxette's car with the Queensland number plates, and Roxette was getting into the Range Rover.

"Where d'you think you're going?" she asked.

"To make sure he doesn't bottle it," said Roxette, turning on the ignition.

Valerie wasn't sure she knew what 'bottle it' meant, but it didn't sound good.

"No, no, you can't go," she said.

The last thing she wanted was for Roxette to realise that Rory was going to kill his brother rather than rob a bank.

"I need the Range Rover," she added, lamely.

"Use your own car," said Roxette. "You remember my password on the computer?"

"Yes," said Valerie, suspiciously. Why was Roxette asking? Had she found out Valerie had been using her social media pages?

She needn't have worried.

"I've left three yoga meditation and exercise videos on the computer of Rory and me. Post one on our website every day to give us an alibi."

"Why do you need an alibi?" Valerie demanded.

"I'm following Rory," said Roxette, putting the Range Rover into drive and roaring out of the driveway with a spray of gravel.

Valerie had to jump to avoid being pebble-dashed. She stood there yelling at Roxette to stop. She didn't like the idea of Roxette following Rory. Not one bit. She might interfere; stop him from killing Mike. God knows he was nervous enough; he wouldn't take much dissuading. Her shouts were in vain, Roxette was already out through the farm gate and speeding north.

Valerie stood there, swearing under her breath, then she started yelling,

"Shit. Shit. Shit!"

She wondered if she should phone Rory and warn him. But would that make things worse? Rattle him even more? He'd probably call the whole thing off.

She decided she would have to risk it. They couldn't have Roxette as a witness to the murder. She went into the house, picked up her mobile phone, tapped in the speed dial, held it to her ear and waited.

She could hear it ringing.

Actually, she could hear it ringing twice: once through the phone; once from her bedroom.

She walked into the bedroom. There was Rory's phone.

When Roxette had woken him with coffee and an upper, she'd told him not to take his mobile phone with him; it could be traced. If things went wrong, the police would know where he'd been. So Rory had dutifully left his phone by the bedside. Valerie couldn't contact him now, even if she wanted to. All she could do was wait, keep her fingers crossed, and post a video on the website each day. Well, every other day, because she knew it would take about five days to complete the task.

Despite driving a car with Queensland number plates, Rory didn't want to go through the police checkpoint on the Queensland/New South Wales border near the Gold Coast. The police were unlikely to stop him but he didn't want them to have any record of him crossing the border when they found his brother's blood-soaked body in Queensland.

He was hoping to prove that he had never left New South Wales. So, he avoided the Pacific Highway north and instead drove inland through Kyogle and Grevillia and up the winding road onto the plateau on the other side of the Great Divide, intending to cross the border near Legume, far from the eyes of the police.

Roxette's car was a Subaru Liberty. Rory had bought it for her. She had wanted a WRX but Rory had baulked at the price. Now he was sorry he had. He would have enjoyed roaring through the winding roads in the WRX; especially since the effects of the upper that Roxette had given him earlier still hadn't worn off.

No matter; with practically no traffic and the Liberty's all-wheel-drive gripping the corners, he still felt like Lewis Hamilton.

Further back, in the Range Rover, Roxette wasn't enjoying the ride quite as much.

The Range Rover was more luxurious, but the suspension was a bit softer, giving it a slight floating feeling when she took the really tight corners at speed. She began to feel a little woozy.

In the end, she decided she didn't need to speed. Her GPS told her where Rory was. She didn't need to keep up with him. She eased back on the accelerator. The Range Rover stopped tilting and rolling on the corners. Instead, it slid through, smoothly taking the steep gradients and gliding up the escarpment.

Valerie had planned for Rory to take three days to travel north. Sleeping in the car, he would get to Mike's house early on the third day. All he had to do then was wait for Mary to go to work before making his move. That meant he would be anything up to five hours back down the road south, before Mary got home and found Mike's body.

Rory, on the other hand, had no intention of sleeping in the car.

If things went wrong, he could be sleeping on a hard prison bunk for the next few years. This would be his last chance of luxury, so he planned to stay in the best hotels he could find, in the largest towns he could find. He reckoned nobody would remember him anyway, and if he paid cash there would be no electronic record of his stay.

He'd planned to stay the first night in Gladstone but he was a little worried when he got away later than he'd expected. Would he get that far before nightfall? He needn't have worried. With the Covid lockdown, the roads were almost empty and there were no road works. Half way through the day he was sure he would comfortably reach his destination.

Mary had left home long before Rory. She'd planned to do the journey to Northern New South Wales in just two days, rather than three. She intended doing this by catnapping in the campervan every few hours and driving right through the night. She was in a hurry. She needed to clear Mike's name and destroy Rory's and Valerie's reputation before anybody noticed that Mike was missing.

She'd managed quite well with just a few hours' sleep on the side of the road during the first night; even so, by the time she reached Gladstone, she knew she wouldn't get to Lismore until after dark.

She phoned John. Firstly, to tell him she was running late. Secondly to make sure he was on the road to Lismore himself.

He confirmed that he was, then told her the name of the motel where he'd booked a room.

"It'll be dark before I get there," said Mary, "Don't wait for me, if you want something to eat."

"Don't know what I'll get in Lismore, with all the restaurants shut because of the virus," John grumbled.

Then, remembering that she held the threat of maybe getting him fined, or even sent to prison, he decided to be a little more friendly.

"Do you want me to book you a room at the motel?" he asked.

"That won't be necessary," said Mary, "Just expect me when you see me but I'll definitely be there tonight. We've got an appointment with the beehive maker first thing tomorrow morning. Then the bank manager."

"Look," said John, "What's this all about? Why do you need me to see the bee hive people? Or the bank manager? Why can't Mike do it?"

"Mike's allergic to bee stings," Mary said truthfully but obliquely.

"Well why keep bees in the first place, then?" asked John.

But he got no answer. Mary had hung up. She had also been distracted.

As she drove through Gladstone, she was sure she saw Rory's Range Rover parked opposite a hotel. It certainly looked like Rory's car. She couldn't remember Rory's registration number but it had New South Wales number plates. What was Rory doing up here?

Then she relaxed. A woman was sitting in the Range Rover and it definitely wasn't Valerie. She was blonde with her hair pulled back and she was wearing a rather masculine shirt.

Mary sped past the parked Range Rover without the driver even glancing in Mary's direction. She seemed to be staring intently ahead at the large hotel further up the road.

Mary made just one more pit stop before she got into the northern suburbs of Brisbane and took the road to the airport and the city by-pass. She filled up with petrol, had a snack and washed her face in the service station restrooms, but although she was tired, she couldn't sleep, so she decided to drive on.

Even so, as she'd predicted, it was dark when she reached the Lismore motel. There was only one car in the motel carpark and it wasn't the car John had driven up to Mary and Mike's place a few weeks earlier. Mary wondered if John had changed his mind and not bothered to come at all. What would she do then? She parked the campervan alongside the other car and called him on his mobile. He answered on almost the first ring.

"Where are you?" Mary asked anxiously.

"At the motel."

"What room number?"

"This one," he answered.

He had heard the campervan parking and had stepped out of his room to investigate. Now he was standing right in front of her, waving at her through the windscreen.

She hung up and climbed out of campervan. As her feet hit the ground she stumbled slightly. Driving for almost twenty hours straight had caused her legs to stiffen up.

John moved forward to catch her.

"Are you alright?"

She pulled away from his outstretched hand.

"I'm fine," she said. Then to change the subject she added, "That's not the car you had before."

"No," said John, "I sold the other one to a bloke in a pub."

Suspecting that this might make him think there was nothing to connect him to the break-in at the abattoir, Mary said, "They'll still be able to trace it to you through the registration."

"No," said John, "I bought it from a bloke in a pub, as well. I never bothered to put the registration in my name."

"Why do I get the idea that you're disreputable?" asked Mary, and she walked into John's motel room.

"Disreputable? Listen to the baby-faced blackmailer."

Unlike Rory, John hadn't bothered to waste money on the best accommodation he could find. The room was in a typical country motel. A double bed, a small table and one chair, a small bar fridge and a huge flat TV Screen on the wall.

Mary plonked herself into the chair.

John looked at her carefully. She was obviously exhausted. He'd brought a bottle of scotch with him and he poured Mary a generous slug. She swallowed the lot in one go while John was refilling his glass. He topped her glass up again.

"Thanks," she said.

"No worries," he said.

He sat on the bed opposite her.

"So, are you going to tell me what this is all about? What are we doing here? Why isn't Mike here?"

Mary took a deep breath, but she resisted the temptation to swallow the second glass of scotch.

"Mike's dead," she said.

"Dead?" John repeated. It occurred to him that all he seemed to be able to do was repeat what she said. "How?"

"I told you, he's allergic to bee stings. He was stung to death."

"So why are we here? Why are you buying a bee hive?"

Mary sipped her drink. She'd been thinking about what she would or wouldn't tell him all the way down from Cairns, but now the time had come she needed to choose her words carefully.

"Mike's dad was a real bastard," she started. "When he died, he left a will that said neither of his sons would inherit anything until the other one was dead. Then the surviving brother would get everything."

"So, you don't want people to know Mike's dead until you get the inheritance?" John guessed.

"No," snapped Mary, "I don't care about the money. I care about Mike's reputation. His brother and sister-in-law have been involved in a fraud. When Mike wouldn't cover for them, they started trolling him, claiming he was a paedophile. Half the Queensland Education Department believe he is. My school won't even let me have contact with my students online in case that puts them in danger. I want Mike's name cleared. I want my name cleared. I want everybody to know Rory and Valerie are responsible. I want them charged with fraud. Then I can bury Mike in peace."

There was a moment's pause and John absorbed this and Mary gulped at her scotch.

"So where do I come in?" John finally asked.

"I want you to pretend to be Mike. Just long enough to

see the bank manager about the fraud. I've got some hair clippers in the van and Mike's driving licence and credit cards. With a haircut and shave you'll look just like him."

"Not that much like him," protested John.

"Near enough," said Mary, "Nobody up here knows Mike except Rory and Valerie and we won't be going anywhere near them. The bank manager has never met Mike, nor has the bee hive maker or the police…"

"Police?" John broke in. There he was again; repeating what she said.

"You have to report the trolling. You have to report the fraud. The will has nothing to do with me. I can't report them."

"Geez," John said, "You wouldn't read about it, would you?"

Mary took him literally.

"You might have, if Mike had lived long enough," she said, "He was threatening to write a book about his family."

John swallowed his drink, re-filled it and offered to top up Mary's glass. She put her hand over the glass to stop him.

He sat back down on the bed, thinking about it, then he said, "You know my dad was Mike's dad's older brother, don't you?"

"Older?" queried Mary, since both Mike and Rory were older than John.

"Yes," said John. "Paddy was his little brother. They both ended up in an orphanage in Liverpool after the war. Paddy had a terrible time. He was probably dyslexic; anyway, he couldn't read or write. The nuns at the orphanage used to belt him for it. Nothing my father could do. He wasn't much older than Paddy. Then Paddy was sent to

Australia. He must have had an even worse time here."

"Not according to him," said Mary, "He reckoned he just walked in through the front door of the orphanage, out through the back, over the wall and went to work on the Snowy Mountain Scheme."

"He might have done that later, but not when he first arrived. Dad said he was no more than ten at the time. He wouldn't be the first person to lie about being abused. Too ashamed to admit it happened."

Mary had only seen Paddy when he was in bed and when he was laid out in his coffin. Even then he had looked strong, angry. She found it difficult to imagine him as a frightened little boy.

"That's probably what made him hard," John continued, "Made him turn against his own family. Imagine having two sons at university when you can't even read or write. My dad came to Australia later, as a ten-pound-pom, to try and find Paddy. By that time Paddy was a successful builder. Told my dad to bugger off. He wasn't there when Paddy needed him. He needn't come around looking for a hand-out now."

"He must have been very bitter," said Mary, "Very lonely."

"Yeah. My dad never saw him again. Didn't even know he was dead until I asked about him."

"He died unloved and un-mourned," said Mary, "I don't want that happening to Mike. I don't want his memory stained."

John nodded. He understood, but he was still looking out for his own interests.

"When this is all over," he asked, "Can I write a book about it?"

"When it's all over," said Mary, "You can do what you

bloody well like."

"Great," said John, already wondering whether he should write the book as a supposedly fictional novel or a 'warts and all' exposé. He decided on the exposé; that way he could write it in the first person and make himself the hero.

Mary slept in the campervan parked outside John's motel room. John offered to let her use the bed while he slept in the van, but she'd refused. In a way, John was grateful. It gave him time to research flow hives, the trolls of Valerie and Roxette, bee keeping in general and fraud in particular; all in thorough preparation for the following day but also essential for his future book.

In fact, he was so excited about the idea of the book that he woke Mary with a cup of tea and toast and made sure she was showered and dressed in time for their appointments; firstly, at the Free-Flow Beehive Company then at the bank and finally, the police station.

John left his car in a corner of the motel carpark after checking with the management that it was okay by them. Mary had cut his hair in the style Mike wore, and trimmed his beard. If the motel management noticed, they didn't say anything. In any event they weren't going to complain about John leaving his car there. They certainly didn't need the car space; they had no other bookings, and the fact that John would return later to collect his car and stay overnight was the best commercial news they'd had in a week.

As Mary drove to the beehive manufacturers, John went into full 'reporter' mode, interviewing Mary and using his phone as a voice recorder. He interviewed her on everything; the trauma of the first time one of Mike's pupils had accused him of molesting her and then the trauma of discovering that Mike had prostate cancer, right through to the time Mike decided to keep bees.

He interviewed her about everything and he remembered everything.

At the bee hive place he was more knowledgeable about bees than Mike had ever been, and when they arrived at the bank, armed with Mike's I.D. and credit cards, and said they were there to see the bank manager, Mary almost felt like John was channelling Mike. Except for the fact that John was far more authoritative and seemingly far more angry about Rory and Valerie using his father's Trust as security against a loan.

He was also far more aware of the ramifications of the loan, both for Rory and Valerie, and for the Bank Manager. It was obvious that Rory and Valerie wouldn't be able to make the repayments for the next few months at least, and possibly never. And as John pointed out, the Bank could never recoup the money through taking possession of the Retreat, because the Retreat was on land owned by the Trust.

John also insisted on telling 'his' story to both the Bank Manager and the Chief Accountant, because obviously somebody had messed up by giving Rory the loan without checking the title deeds on the land, so John wanted a witness; somebody whose head wouldn't roll when it was discovered that the loan was given without the deeds to the property being checked properly.

Mary realized that this was a very good ploy when John mentioned that Rory and Valerie didn't actually own the farm at the time they took out the mortgage. The Bank Manager went positively puce and the female Chief Accountant looked like the cat that got the cream.

By the time John and Mary left the bank, they were

convinced that Rory and Valerie were in deep trouble, but just to make doubly sure, they headed straight for the local police station to make a complaint about Valerie's trolling. It would be an exaggeration to say the Desk Sergeant showed much enthusiasm for their complaint.

"It's not really our concern," he said, "Maybe you should report it to the administrators or the site owners or someone."

He was referring to the operators of the social pages.

"Don't you think we've tried?" asked Mary. "They do nothing. And anyway the trolls just pop up again on some other site. I'm a teacher. They're claiming my husband and I are paedophiles."

"Sorry I can't help you," said the Sergeant, not sounding sorry at all.

"But the trolls live in your area," said John, "Valerie and Rory Maguire, up on the Maguire macadamia plantation. They're just using fictitious names. The latest one is Roxette Simpson, for god's sake."

"No, Roxette Simpson's not a fictitious name," said the young Constable working nearby, "She was in here the other day asking about a gun licence. Apparently, they're having vermin problems up on the macadamia farm now that nobody's working the place because of Covid. She gave the Maguire plantation as her address, but."

"Well, there you are then," said the Sergeant. "Seems you've got all the information you need to go to the education department; clear your names."

"Thanks for nothing," said Mary, and she walked out.

"Sorry, Sergeant," said John, "Can I have your names? Please?"

"Why?" asked the Sergeant, with a frown.

"To put in my report," said John, reasonably, "I'm a

reporter."

"In that case, no, you can't," said the Sergeant. "Bugger off."

"No worries," said John, holding up the phone he'd been recording the conversation with, "I've got your badge numbers, anyway."

Mary was waiting impatiently when John came out of the police station,

"Well that was a waste of time," she said,

"I dunno," said, John. "At least you know for sure who's behind the trolling."

"I knew already," said Mary.

"Sure," said John, not wanting to get into an argument. "Can you drive me back to the motel?"

"Oh, that's it for you, is it?" asked Mary.

"No," said John, "I just need to get my suitcase; I'm coming up to Cairns with you."

Mary realized she was being unreasonable.

"That's very kind of you, but I can't ask you to drive all the way up there."

"I've got to," said John, "I've only got half a story, so far. Not enough to write a book."

He headed towards the passenger door and waited for Mary to unlock the door of the campervan.

As they got into the van, John asked, "How well does your school principal know Mike?"

"Not at all," said Mary. "They've never met."

"Good," said John, "I'll talk to her as well. She should make a good chapter."

Meanwhile Valerie was alone at the farmhouse, grappling with the complexities of transferring Roxette's first video onto the Retreat's web page. She had both Rory's and her own mobile phones, lying on the desk beside her, ready to intercept any calls Rory might get.

Suddenly Rory's phone started ringing: *"The Ride of the Valkyries"* although Valerie knew it only as the theme music from *"Apocalypse Now".*

The music seemed strangely apt when Valerie picked up the phone and read the name of the caller.

'*Bank Manager,*' it read.

Valerie wondered what to do. Should she answer it? Should she just let it ring out? Eventually she did nothing and the phone stopped ringing. Relieved, she had just put the phone down when a shrill '*beeep!*' cut the air, advising her that Rory had a voice message.

Valerie stared at the phone, then picked it up and went to voice mail. The surprisingly friendly voice of the Bank Manager came on.

"Rory," he said, as if Rory was his greatest friend in the world, "How are you coping with this Covid nonsense? It's driving a lot of people to the wall I can tell you. Fortunately, we're here to help. I'm happy to tell you that the six month's moratorium on your loan repayments we were talking about has been approved. We're doing it for just our best customers. Give me a call and let me know if you'd like to take up the offer."

The phone went dead.

Valerie sat there stunned. She couldn't believe her luck. They had a six-month stay of sentence. Maybe it wasn't necessary for Rory to kill Mike after all. In fact, if he knew about it, Valerie was sure that Rory would think it wasn't necessary.

"Only one thing to do," thought Valerie; "Don't tell him."

"Besides," she told herself, "He doesn't have his mobile with him. I couldn't call him even if I wanted to."

Valerie wasn't the only one keeping secrets. The Bank Manager and his Chief Accountant had their own secrets to keep.

The Chief Accountant was about ten years younger than Valerie, but life hadn't been so kind to her. Too long sitting at her desk at the bank had widened her bottom, and too many disappointments had shrunken her heart. She and the Bank Manager had been carrying on an affair for more than a decade. The best years of her life, as she constantly reminded herself. She had passed up promotions and transfers to other branches of the bank to be with him. He had always said he would leave his wife when their children had grown up, but the youngest child was at university now; about to graduate if Covid didn't get in the way and delay her studies.

The Chief Accountant knew the Bank Manager would never leave his wife. He was too afraid of her. The Chief Accountant was facing a bleak future, growing old alone while the Bank Manager and his wife enjoyed the benefits of his Bank Manager's salary, and his generous superannuation package.

Despite this, the Chief Accountant now sat, smiling to herself, wishing she could see the Bank Manager's wife's face when she learned what had happened. She couldn't help enjoying her superior's discomfort. There would be no Bank Manager's nice salary; no generous superannuation package. Not once this got out.

"What a pity you didn't check the property deeds before making that loan," she said, trying not to sound smug.

But the Bank Manager hadn't managed to string her along for more than a dozen years without being extremely devious.

"Yes," he agreed, "Especially now. Just when the kids are all gone and I could finally divorce Heather and we could be together. Not much fun being together if I'm out of work."

She knew why he said it. Knew he was manipulating her again. But did it matter? She also knew she had his balls in a vice and if he tried to wriggle out of leaving his wife this time, she would happily turn the screws.

"Well," she said, smiling sweetly, "I guess nobody has to know for a little while, not while you're going through a divorce."

CHAPTER NINETEEN

While the Bank Manager was building up the courage to tell his wife that he was leaving her, and Mary and John were picking up his luggage and driving north over the Queensland border, Roxette was still sitting in the Range Rover just down the street from Rory's hotel in Gladstone.

She had been there since the previous morning, waiting to follow him. But he hadn't appeared and Roxette was beginning to worry,

Eventually she decided to phone Valerie.

Valerie was relieved to hear from her; it would give her a chance to stop Roxette following Rory.

"Where are you?" she asked, "Are you still following Rory? There's no need."

Roxette ignored her. Gangster's Molls don't listen to people's wives.

"Is Gladstone the place the bank manager lives?" she asked.

For a moment Valerie didn't understand what Roxette was talking about; then she remembered.

"No, no," she said. "It's miles north of there."

"Then, why is Rory still sitting in his hotel room in Gladstone?" asked Roxette. "He's pretty scared. He's not going to bottle it, is he? Even worse, top himself?"

"No, no," said Valerie.

"Then why is he still in the hotel? Maybe I should go in and check on him."

"No," said Valerie. "What's the name of the hotel? I'll

call him."

Rory was sitting in his hotel room watching daytime TV. Not that he liked daytime TV; he was just too terrified to move. Too afraid that when the time came, he wouldn't be able to pull the trigger. The effect of the upper that Roxette had given him had long worn off and he was just left with a jumpy feeling, made worse when his room telephone suddenly began to ring.

He stared at the phone, afraid to answer it. Then he calmed himself. It must just be the hotel reception asking if he was staying another night. Nobody else knew he was there.

He picked up the phone and immediately realised his mistake.

"What the hell are you doing still in Gladstone?" Valerie asked, not even bothering to identify herself or inquire after his health.

"How did you know I was here?" he asked, ignoring her question, "Are you following me?"

"Not me," said Valerie, "Roxette."

Rory couldn't believe it.

"Bloody Roxette, she thinks this is all a bloody game. Why did you let her follow me?" he demanded, "She could spoil everything!"

"I couldn't stop her," said Valerie, "Besides it might be a good thing she is following you if you're still cowering in your hotel room."

Then she added the twist of the knife.

"The Bank Manager called. He wants you to call him. Go in and see him about the loan,"

Then she added the lie that she thought would push him on up the coast.

"He asked that you bring in the deeds of the farm when

you go to see him."

It had the required effect.

"Shit," said Rory, convinced that the game was up.

"It's okay," said Valerie, "I told him you were away for the week on business. By then Mike will be dead. You'll own the whole farm… That is if you're not going to bottle it."

Unlike Valerie, Rory had heard the expression before.

"I'm not going to bottle anything," he said, although up until the time Valerie called him, that had been a real possibility. Now he was really convinced that he had no choice. The Bank Manager had produced the ticking clock. Mike had to be dead within the next week.

"Where's Roxette now?" he asked.

"Watching the hotel, I guess," said Valerie.

"I've got her car," said Rory.

"She took the Range Rover. She just waited until you'd driven out of sight, then she jumped in the Range Rover and roared off."

"Well, how did she follow me?" Rory asked.

Even though Rory obviously couldn't see her, Valerie shrugged.

"There aren't that many roads north."

Then Rory remembered. He was driving Roxette's car. He remembered insisting that it was fitted with a theft-proof locator so she wouldn't lose it.

Suddenly he felt quite calm. For the first time since he first woke up with a hangover to learn that Valerie was taking the plan to kill Mike seriously, he felt in control.

"Tell Roxette to meet me outside the hotel in twenty minutes," he said, and headed off for the shower.

Rory almost looked like a new man as he strode out of the hotel. He wasn't expecting this new-found confidence to necessarily last long enough to kill Mike, but for the moment he had a plan and he was in control.

He stood waiting outside the hotel, holding his duffle bag in one hand and Roxette's car keys in the other.

As she drove up and parked alongside him, he waved her car keys in the air.

"You want to swap keys?" he asked her, as she got out of the Range Rover.

"Why?" asked Roxette.

"I know you've got an anti-theft locator in your car," he said, "I know you can trace me wherever I go, on your phone."

Apparently reluctantly, Roxette swapped keys and Rory went to the back of the Range Rover to pull out her suitcase and put his duffle-bag in.

"I'll leave the camping equipment in your car," he said, mostly to show that he was in control, "I won't be needing it. I'll be staying first class all the way."

Roxette said nothing; still apparently conceding that Rory was in control. He pointed back down the road heading south, the way they had both come.

"Now you just turn around and head back to the farm." he said, "I'm going north and I'll stop somewhere on the road, and if I see you following me, the robbery is off. There'll be no robbery, no money, no Topaz Retreat. Understand?"

"Yes," said Roxette, almost inaudibly.

Rory opened the driver's side door of the Range Rover then stopped.

"That tablet," he said, "The one you gave me when I woke up with a hangover, what was it?"

"Paracetamol," she said.

"Bullshit," said Rory, "Paracetamol doesn't work like

that. Give me a couple more…make it three."

Again with apparent reluctance,, Roxette handed over the pills. Grinning, Rory popped one of the pills into his mouth and started chewing it. Then he put the other two pills into his pocket, got into the Range Rover, and roared away.

Roxette didn't move until he was out of sight. Then she got into her Subaru and started the engine.

She switched on the GPS and logged into 'Recent Journeys.'

There, sure enough, was an address near Cairns.

She hadn't put the location in her GPS so it must have been Rory. It seemed to be a bit out in the bush, so she didn't think it would be the actual bank. It must be where the bank manager lived.

Despite now knowing exactly where Rory was going, she did as she was told, turned the car around and headed south.

There was a service station and fast-food takeaway joint just a few miles south of town. She filled the car with petrol then sat in the car, eating a lazy brunch. She was in no hurry. She was pretty sure that Rory would be doing the same thing maybe a hundred kilometres further north. He'd fill his Range Rover, eat his lunch sitting in his car, watching the road to make sure she wasn't following.

Roxette knew Rory wasn't a patient man. She knew he wouldn't wait forever. Twenty minutes and he'd be twitchy, especially after chewing the upper. Half an hour and he'd be giving up and heading north again, convinced that she wasn't following.

She'd give him an hour. Then she'd drive steadily north. She was pretty sure Rory would stop when it got dark. She'd overtake him when he was either already in bed or enjoying room service.

She'd stop much later, camp by the roadside, wake much earlier. She'd be at his destination long before him. She could check out the place, then wait for him and make sure he didn't mess it all up. And just to make sure Rory wouldn't suspect that she was still tailing him, Roxette phoned Valerie and told her what had happened.

"If Rory phones," she told Valerie, "Tell him I'm driving back to the farm. If he phones after it's dark, tell him I'm already there, but I'm sleeping."

"And what time will you be back?" Valerie asked.

"I won't," said Roxette, "I'm not going to miss this. This is way better than acting or being a bloody shaman."

CHAPTER TWENTY

Roxette arrived at Mary and Mike's property early the following morning. It looked an unlikely home for a bank manager. Miles from anywhere. No front gate and a driveway disappearing into the rainforest that ran along both sides of the roadway. No neighbours, and only the occasional open field or pasture. There weren't even any buildings visible from the road on the property listed on Roxette's GPS.

She wondered if perhaps Rory had put a false address into the GPS to mislead her.

She quickly dismissed the idea.

Firstly, because he had only learnt that she was following him a few minutes before he appeared and reclaimed the Range Rover. Roxette had her eyes on her vehicle all that time so he couldn't have nipped out and loaded in a false address.

Secondly, because, well, he was just too bloody stupid to think of anything that clever.

She drove back along the road and past the property; peering down the driveway but seeing nothing but trees. She pulled into the side of the road. All she could do now was wait and hope Rory turned up sooner or later.

It occurred to her that she couldn't wait where she was. Rory would have to drive past that spot to reach the property. He might spot the car. She decided to drive past the property again and park amongst the trees somewhere further up the road.

She quickly found the ideal spot. She could drive into

the trees, where she could still see the entrance to the property but be hidden from view for anybody driving up the road, or in and out of the property.

She settled down to wait. Then she decided she would better occupy her time *'casing the joint'* as they say in old gangster movies. She was now even thinking in gangster clichés.

She removed a .22 Rifle from her suit case and loaded it. Then she started making her way towards the property; not down the driveway but through the trees.

It was hot and Roxette was a city girl not used to the bush, which was full of strange sounds and smells. She could hear insects buzzing around in the heat. The air was heavily scented.

Then she stopped. She knew that smell. She moved off to the side, through the bush, and suddenly came upon the marijuana plantation. The marijuana was planted under the rainforest trees, obviously to avoid aerial sur-veillance. They towered over Roxette so that she couldn't see the far side of the plantation; it seemed to go on for-ever.

Roxette was now even more confused. Why would a bank manager be growing marijuana? Then she remem-bered that it was Valerie not Rory who had said he was robbing a bank. Maybe Rory wasn't robbing a bank at all. Maybe he was robbing some drug dealers.

It made sense.

Of course, it was more dangerous robbing drug dealers. Roxette knew a couple of them from the Gold Coast and they carried guns. On the other hand, if Rory got away with it, he was home free. The drug dealers could hardly go to the police and report the robbery.

One thing was for sure, if Rory did intend to rob some

drug dealer, he would need Roxette's help more than ever. So, she continued *'casing the joint'*; finding the lie of the land.

After the end of the marijuana plantation, the bush got slightly thicker for a while, then opened up onto a roughly mown lawn in front of a large, single-storey Queenslander house with a veranda all the way around on three sides. On the fourth side was a large shed or garage, almost as big as the house itself.

As she waited on the edge of the bush, Roxette became aware of bees buzzing around. She searched for the source of the buzzing. In the clearing, next to the trees, stood a domestic beehive. Beside it, on the ground, was a box with a hole in the side covered with netting. Not that the netting kept any of the bees inside the box because the box lid was off, and a saucer of something very attractive to bees had been placed on the beehive.

Roxette didn't know it, but this was Mary's attempt to persuade the swarm to move into the beehive. Mary had no idea how to do it, so she had just placed sugar water inside and outside the hive, left the box open beside the hive and left the rest to the bees. It seemed to be working because in the days that she had been away the Queen bee had found its way into the hive; hence all the activity as the colony starting to settle in.

Roxette didn't like bees so she gave them a wide berth, moved further back into the bush, and found a vantage point from which she could study the house. There were no cars parked beside the property but the shed was large enough to hold three or four vehicles. Unlike the shed, the house seemed to be surrounded almost entirely in glass.

She was just considering whether it was safe to take a closer look to see if there were any vehicles parked in the shed, and therefore people in the house, when she heard, or thought she heard, a powerful car engine drive up and stop on the road near the property.

Gripping her rifle tightly, Roxette made her way silently back through the trees, parallel with the driveway, until she could see the road.

She couldn't see anything as she approached but she could hear the high-pitched whine of a car reversing.

Then she heard the sound of branches cracking, leaves rustling, and an engine being switched off.

She moved to the edge of the bush to get a better look. She could just make out Rory's Range Rover amongst the trees. She couldn't see Rory, but she could hear him.

He had backed his Range Rover into the trees so that it couldn't easily be seen from the road. It wasn't as well hidden as Roxette's vehicle but it was parked with its nose pointing out to the road for a quick getaway. What Roxette could hear was the sound of Rory getting out of the Range Rover and pushing his way through the bush to the back of the vehicle.

Roxette crouched down, hiding behind a small barrel set on a fencepost, at the junction of the road and the driveway. Obviously, it served as the property's post-box.

As she crouched, her eyes came level with the name on the barrel:

M & M Maguire.

It didn't take Roxette a millisecond to put two and two together. This couldn't be a coincidence. This had to be Rory's brother's house. And Roxette doubted that Rory was here to rob him. More likely to kill him. Then his father's Trust would belong to Rory.

No wonder he had been so nervous. Roxette was willing to bet this was all Valerie's idea. And Valerie had made damn sure that she would be far away when the murder took place.

Oblivious to Roxette's presence, Rory took the sawn-off shotgun out of his duffle bag and loaded both barrels. Then he put a few spare shells into his pocket, took one of the uppers out of his pocket and started chewing. He was already wearing leather driving gloves to avoid any fingerprints on the shotgun. He pulled on a balaclava, pulling the bottom of the face-hole up to form a mask. As he stepped out into the driveway, wearing the balaclava and gripping the shot-gun as if he knew how to use it, he looked quite scary.

From her hiding place, Roxette was so excited that she shivered involuntarily.

Taking a deep breath and holding his sawn-off shotgun with both hands, Rory started making his way cautiously down the driveway.

Because the driveway was curved it was impossible to see both ends at the same time. He looked down the driveway then turned and looked back up the driveway to make sure he wasn't being followed. But he didn't look into the rainforest on the other side of the driveway where Roxette was lying low, waiting for him to pass. He moved within a few feet of her, completely unaware of her presence.

She let him pass then took one of the nylon stockings out of her pocket and pulled it over her head. Now she looked even scarier than Rory. Satisfied, she began following him as quietly as she could, moving through the bush. This was slow going and she lost sight of him for a while. Then she almost bumped into him. He had stopped and stepped into the bush himself.

As Roxette had done a few minutes before, Rory was

watching the house for any signs of life or movement. There was nothing. Not even a dog barking. Not that he'd expected a dog. He knew Mike was scared of dogs.

Eventually Rory tip-toed quickly across the open ground between the bush and the house; then he flattened himself against the shed wall and peered around the corner. Most of the verandas had sliding glass doors. Anybody approaching would easily be seen by someone inside. Rory also noticed there were sensors and lights all around the house. They might not be switched on during the day but he wasn't taking any chances. He needed a way into the house that didn't involve walking on the veranda.

There was a door in the side of the shed where Rory was standing. Rory tried the door handle. It turned. Looking around to make sure nobody was watching, Rory opened the door, decided the coast was clear, and slipped into the darkness of the shed.

Roxette was afraid that Rory had spotted her when he looked around, but relaxed when it became obvious he hadn't. She wondered what to do. She decided to stay hidden. If Rory was discovered, she would need the element of surprise to rescue him and finish the job.

Inside the shed, Rory's eyes were just getting used to the darkness. The shed was almost empty. There was just one small hatchback car where a couple of vans could easily park. There was also a commercial-sized chest freezer and a few tools, some of which had been knocked off their hooks and lay on the floor. There was also another door, like the one Rory had entered, which presumably led to inside the house.

Rory carefully crossed the shed and tried the other door.

It was locked.

Cursing softly, Rory retraced his steps and opened the door he'd come in through.

He peered out to make sure the coast was clear.

It was just as well he did because although he saw nothing, he could hear a vehicle coming down the driveway. Holding the door almost closed and peering through the crack, he saw a campervan approaching. It looked like Mary and Mike in the van and Mary was driving. Rory never let Valerie drive when they were in the car together. He was a very nervous passenger. Right now, he was also a very nervous would-be assassin. He pulled the door even closer together until he could just see out of it through a narrow crack.

In the bushes behind the campervan, Roxette quietly put a bullet into the breach of her rifle. There were two people in the van. This is exactly why she had followed Rory. If he stepped out to confront the two of them, she'd take the second person.

But he didn't step out and the people didn't get out of the van.

John and Mary sat in the parked campervan, almost too tired to move. They had been driving continuously for the last few days. All John wanted was a soft bed. All Mary wanted was a hot bath, and then a soft bed.

"Do you want me to take the beehive out of the back of the van?" John asked, because he felt he should but hoped she'd say no.

She did.

"Leave it," she said, "When the time comes, I'm going to take it up to the Daintree with the other beehive and Mike's body. When they find his body, they'll think he died up there."

"Provided his body has thawed out before they find it," said John, rather thoughtlessly.

Mary glowered at him.

"You can have the same bedroom you had last time," she said, and picking up the remote control, she pressed it and waited patiently for the tilt door on the shed to open.

CHAPTER TWENTY-ONE

Inside the shed, Rory realized he was trapped. The smart thing to do would have been to burst out of the side door and run like hell across the lawn and into the bush before either Mike or Mary had time to react. But Rory wasn't that smart. Besides he didn't want them to see a man with a balaclava and shotgun running across their lawn. The first thing they'd do is call the police. Then it would be impossible to try to stage Mike's suicide.

Rory looked around in panic. Where could he hide? Behind the car?

He rushed to the car. It was a little compact model, it hardly seemed to offer any cover. The garage door was beginning to open. He looked around again.

The chest freezer.

It was certainly big enough to hide in. The cold wouldn't matter, he'd only be there until Mike and Mary had gone into the house.

Holding his shotgun in one hand, he swung open the chest freezer lid with the other.

He had already got one leg up onto the side of the freezer and was about to dive in when he looked down.

There, staring back up at him was Mike's swollen face.

Rory didn't recognize his brother, but he did recognize a dead body.

He screamed, and fell backwards as he lost his footing.

The shotgun fired.

It was pointing up at the ceiling. If it had been a normal shotgun, the pellets would have all harmlessly blasted a small hole in the ceiling but, being a sawn-off shotgun, the spray of pellets spread wider, catching Rory's face and shredding part of the balaclava.

It didn't kill him, but that's where his luck ended.

The impact threw him backwards onto the ground, straight onto the enormous scythe lying there. The impact of his body, falling onto the blade, almost cut his head off.

In the campervan, John and Mary sat bolt upright.

"What the hell was that?" demanded John, but he made no attempt to get out of the campervan to find out.

Behind the campervan, still hidden in the bush and gripping her rifle, Roxette was wondering the same thing.

The tilt door was fully up now but the interior of the shed was still in semi-darkness.

Mary switched on the campervan headlights to illuminate the scene. They could just make out Rory lying on his back, but not quite on the ground because the scythe was holding his head and shoulders aloft.

"Is that a body?" Mary asked.

"It's not Mike, is it?" asked John.

"Of course, it bloody isn't," said Mary. "Do you think I'd just leave him lying on the ground?... He's in the freezer."

She got out of the campervan. John reluctantly followed.

From the bushes, Roxette strained to see what was going on but the campervan blocked her view.

Mary moved forward cautiously, followed by an even more cautious John.

"Who is it?" asked John, as they stared down at the almost decapitated head and the blood seeping in a pool underneath it.

The balaclava had been shredded by the shotgun blast. It waved in the breeze, but Mary still couldn't see Rory's face. She tentatively pulled back the woollen material. The pellets had made a bit of a mess of the face but Mary thought she recognized it. She quickly let go of the balaclava and straightened up.

"I think it's Mike's brother, Rory," said Mary.

"Well," said John, "he's not going to be trolling Mike, now, is he?"

"That's not funny" said Mary.

"No, sorry," said John. "We'd better call the police."

"We can't," said Mary, through clenched teeth, "Mike's body's in the freezer."

"Sorry," said John, again. "So, what do we do now?"

"Let's get out of here," said Mary, and she led the way out of the shed, activating the automatic door on the way out, so that it closed behind them.

Still crouched in her hiding place, Roxette was as confused as Mary and John. She'd never met Mike or Mary, but the name on the post-box said Maguire, and the man looked like a younger version of Rory. It had to be Mike. But what were they doing?

She pulled out her mobile phone, but couldn't see the controls through the stocking on her head. She pushed the stocking up so that it looked like a beanie or maybe a Sikh turban. She switched the phone to silent mode, cursing herself for not doing that earlier. It could have been a fatal mistake. Well, better late than never. She started videoing Mary and John, although from that distance she couldn't pick up much of what they were saying.

In fact, they weren't saying much.

John just stood there. The great writer couldn't think of

a thing. His mind had gone blank.

Mary, however, was thinking hard.

"If Rory's dead," she said eventually, "Then Mike inherits the Trust."

"But Mike's dead," said John.

Mary looked at him as if he was simple.

"He isn't dead until somebody finds his body up in the Daintree alongside his beehives." She said, "We'll take him and the beehives up to the rainforest. Leave him there, then drive back and find the body."

"*This* body," she added, for clarity.

"How do we explain me being here?" asked John, wondering if he hadn't gotten into something out of his depth.

"You've come up to visit Mike. Shouldn't be a problem; the police aren't going to question you. You'll be the least of their worries."

From her hiding place, Roxette continued to video Mary and John as they took their luggage out of the campervan, then disappeared into the house only to re-emerge with a large blanket which Mary proceeded to put over the beehive in the garden. Then she and John carried the beehive to the back of the campervan and shoved it in.

As they passed, Roxette picked up some dialogue.

"Won't the bees suffocate?" John was asking.

"I shouldn't think so," said Mary, "It's a woollen blanket, it isn't airtight. Anyway, it's only while we carry it up to the rainforest."

How long is that going to take?" John asked.

"An hour...hour and a half, tops," said Mary, "Let's get Mike."

Roxette missed this last bit because Mary was re-opening the tilt door and the noise drowned out her voice.

Mary and John disappeared into the shed.

Roxette was now more confused than ever, but she kept videoing. Somehow, she felt certain that there would be a benefit in all this.

Inside the shed, Mary carefully avoided any blood on the floor and opened the freezer door.

"We've got a forklift here somewhere," she said, looking around.

"Don't bother," said John.

He reached in to pick up Mike's body, and then quickly withdrew his hands.

"It's bloody cold," he said.

"Surprise, surprise," said Mary, "I'll get another blanket to wrap him in."

She had the key to the door leading to the house, so she disappeared and quickly returned with the doona off her bed.

John placed the doona over the body. By now the adrenaline had well and truly started pumping. He was the hero of the story again. And what a story! He felt like Superman. He leant into the freezer and tugged Mike free from the ice, then lifted him like a baby, still covered by the doona, and carried him out of the shed and placed him in the back of the campervan.

Roxette's eyes were as big as saucers. Was that Rory's body? It looked too stiff; too rigid. She had to remind herself to keep the phone focused on Mary and John. Again, they were close enough for Roxette to hear them.

"We'll have to leave the campervan up there," Mary was saying. "I'll drive the van; you follow in my car."

"No," said John, still determined to be the hero of his book. The one who took the chances; who drove the body up to the rainforest. It didn't occur to him at the time that this was the part of the story he couldn't write.

"I'll drive the van," he said, "You lead the way in the car. Make sure the road's clear."

John backed the campervan up so Mary could reverse out of the shed. He had no reverse camera so he stopped when he made light contact with the trees. Roxette had to jump to avoid being hit but even as she stumbled back, she kept recording.

Mary reversed out in the narrow confines. She was an expert at it because Mike was always leaving the campervan badly parked. Activating the tilt door closed with one hand, she beeped her horn and drove out onto the road, steering with the other hand.

John's exit was rather more awkward. His three-point turn ended up being a five-point turn and Mary had to wait for him at the end of the driveway. He knew the poor driving was due to nervousness and he tried desperately to get himself under control. Glancing in the rearview mirror he thought he saw something that made him jump with a start: a flash of a figure stepping out into the driveway behind him, wearing a flesh-coloured Parna, or Sikh turban, and holding a mobile phone in front of its face. John couldn't tell if it was a man or a woman.

He blinked. Looked again. There was no-one there. The rear-view vision on the campervan was notoriously bad with no rear-view camera. He must have been mistaken.

He gripped the steering wheel more tightly and concentrated on following Mary up the driveway and out onto the road.

Roxette, now flat to the ground in the bush, was irritated with herself. She had been so preoccupied with videoing events that she had forgotten that the campervan had rear-view mirrors. Still, the campervan hadn't stopped, so she figured the driver hadn't seen her. More important now was finding out what the hell had happened in the shed. She straightened up and dusted herself off. Pocketing her phone but still gripping her rifle, she crossed to the side door of the shed, the one Rory had used to get in.

She wasn't taking much care. She was pretty sure if anybody else was on the property, they would have appeared by now. Once inside the shed, like Rory, her eyes took some time to adjust to the low light. Unlike him, she found the light switch and switched it on.

She turned and gasped.

There was Rory, still lying prone on the scythe, his shotgun by his side. His blood pooling and congealing around him. Flies had started to buzz around.

Roxette stepped forward, making sure not to step in the blood. She took a photo of the body with her phone and considered sending it to Valerie. Then she decided against it. She was sure emailed photos could be traced. Besides what good would telling Valerie do? What good would calling anybody do? Rory had obviously killed himself. Mike and Mary were in the campervan when it happened, so they weren't involved. They obviously had something to hide, but it didn't alter the fact that Mike had now inherited the farm and the Retreat. There would be no share of the Retreat for Roxette; no money.

But, wait. Was that true? Why hadn't Mike and Mary called the police?

Obviously, Roxette concluded, it was the marijuana.

Whatever she'd seen them putting in the campervan was obviously connected with the manufacturing of drugs. They were hiding it before calling the police. But even then, there was a plantation full of the marijuana not more than a hundred yards away. Maybe they intended to harvest that as well? Or hope the police didn't go looking that far?

Well, no way, thought Roxette. She could see now how she could still buy her share of the Retreat.

She looked at the tools still hanging on the wall and scattered on the floor. She picked up the chain saw. Then she found a handful of bin liner bags and headed for the marijuana plantation.

One thing about becoming a Spiritual Healer and Yoga Guru was that it had made Roxette extremely fit. Admittedly she had to discard the stocking on her head and strip down to her bra and jeans to stop overheating, but by the time Mike and Mary had reached the Daintree Forest and started setting out the beehives at Mike's usual campsite, Roxette had already harvested half the plantation.

It was amazing how much marijuana she could cram into a bin liner if she cut the stalks into short pieces. And it was equally amazing how many bin liners she could fit into her Subaru Liberty.

She checked her watch. Mary had said it would take an hour and a half to get to the rainforest. Even if they got there and just dumped what Roxette now thought was a frozen slab of hash, and drove back, it would take three hours minimum.

Roxette intended to give herself two and a half hours to load as much marijuana as she could. After that, she was heading south. Her fortune secured.

CHAPTER TWENTY-TWO

Mary led John off the road into the Daintree Forest and along a bush trail towards the river. Initially, Mike had camped in a public campsite, but after Warren, the indigenous park ranger, had befriended him he had shown him a second, unofficial, more secluded campsite.

It was this campsite that Mary drove to.

She was grateful for the seclusion but with the Covid19 virus forcing all non-essential people into lockdown, there were no tourists around anyway. If the police had stopped her and John on the road up she had planned to tell them they were setting up their bee hives; an essential industry. For that reason, they had hidden Mike's body on a bunk in the back of the campervan and put the beehives right near the door. With the beehives and bees buzzing around, Mary doubted the police would look much further.

In the event, no subterfuge was needed. Mary showed John where Mike usually parked the campervan. They were just unloading the first hive from the back of the campervan when John froze.

He could hear the sound of an engine. It wasn't a car engine. More like an outboard motor for a boat.

Sure enough, Warren in his tinnie, a ten-foot runabout, came chugging around the bend in the river.

John dropped the beehive - fortunately it was the empty free-flow hive - and ducked down behind the campervan.

"Stand up, you fool," Mary hissed, "He knows Mike, he knows the campervan. His name's Warren, give him a wave."

John straightened up and waved.

"G'day, Warren," John called, "How are they biting?"

Warren choked down on the outboard and yelled back, while his boat barely held its position in the strong current.

"Pretty good, no tourists to scare the fish. What are you doing here?"

"Setting up me beehives. All right to leave them here?"

"All right with me. What are you going to do with 'em when they close the Park?"

John had no idea what he was talking about. Had no idea that keeping beehives in the forests of the Daintree National Park would be banned as of 2024.

Mary cut in to save him.

"We'll keep them in our garden," she called.

Warren nodded, revved up the outboard engine and chugged on up the river.

"Come on," said Mary, relieved, "Let's get this hive into the trees."

Holding one end each they shuffled into the trees along the riverbank.

Being a rainforest there was little undergrowth to worry about and they moved deeper into the forest. Now that the adrenaline rush had left him, John no longer felt he had super-human powers. He felt like a middle-aged man doing too much exercise in the tropical heat.

"How much further?" he wheezed.

"Another twenty metres or so," said Mary, "I don't want the hives visible from the campsite, or the river."

"Why not?" asked John, exasperated, and still panting.

Mary seemed to have no trouble carrying her end of the hive while walking and talking.

"Mike was killed next to the beehives," she explained, "We have to leave him there. If they're both in the clearing somebody might find him before he's thawed out."

The thought of carrying Mike's body through the rainforest was a bit much for John.

"Couldn't we just leave him in the campervan?" he asked.

"I'm not a biologist," said Mary, "but I believe bodies give off certain gases and liquids as they thaw. We don't want to leave him in the campervan for a week. Smell the place up. We'd never sell it."

John was slightly shocked at such pragmatism.

"Are you going to sell it?"

"Why would I keep it?" asked Mary. "It was Mike's. Every time I saw it, I'd be reminded of him."

They returned to the campervan after positioning the hive. This time, Mary gave John Mike's beekeeping hat and gloves to wear. She put on her gardening hat and gloves and sprayed them both with insect repellent. It wasn't perfect protection against a hive of bees that were being moved under a blanket, but it was better than nothing.

Mary put the bee smoker on the top of the beehive and they carried the lot into the rainforest and plonked it down a little way from the flow hive. Then, leaving the blanket over the hive to keep the swarm as calm as possible, Mary and John returned once more to the campervan and started to lift Mike's body out.

John couldn't shift it. Mary had to get into the van to help him get the body off the bunk where John had previously put it with apparent ease. At the door, John stopped, dropped Mike's body just inside the door. He thought he was having a heart attack.

"Are you all right?" Mary asked.

"Yeah," he managed to say, taking a few steps towards the river, supposedly to make sure there was nobody about, but in reality to get his breath.

"We could have been in the forest by now," said Mary, "Stop messing about."

Mary took Mike's feet and John his head and they staggered into the forest a third time.

There was a brief discussion about where they should lay Mike. In the end Mary said,

"Just drop him, it'll look more natural."

Mary dropped the feet first, then John gratefully dropped the head.

They both straightened up and looked down at the body.

"Do you think we should say something?" asked John.

"What?" asked Mary.

"I dunno," said John. "Something."

Mary dropped Mike's mobile phone beside the body. The battery was flat by now but he'd had it when he'd died. It had to be there.

After a moment, she bowed her head and joined her hands in front of her as she remembered being taught to do in prayers as a schoolgirl.

Seeing the sign, John bowed his head and clasped his hands.

"Mike, my darling," Mary said, for the first time really thinking about the fact that Mike was actually dead. Tears welled up in her eyes.

"Mike," she repeated, softly, "I know you didn't believe in God or any sort of afterlife. I hope you're right, but if you're not, you've been a good man. A good husband, a good teacher, a good father and grandfather. I'm sure God will let you in. Whatever happens, you can count on one thing; I'm not going to let that bitch of a sister-in-law of yours get away with anything. I'll make sure Matthew and Lucas get everything that should have been yours. Amen."

"Amen," said John, automatically. Then he wondered if it was an entirely appropriate thing to say, and he decided it was. Didn't amen mean *"so be it"*? Well, so be it. John was pretty sure there was only one reason Rory had turned up at Mike's house with a sawn-off shotgun, and that was to kill Mike. No doubt Rory's wife knew about it, too. He was pleased that she wouldn't benefit, even if Rory had been too late and Mike was already dead.

Preoccupied with these thoughts, John turned away from Mike's body and headed for the campervan.

"Oy!" yelled Mary, shattering the mood. "The hat and gloves, leave them here. Mike was wearing them before he died."

John pulled off the hat and gloves.

"Just drop them on the ground," said Mary, as she dropped the bee smoker on the ground beside them and shook the blanket to make sure it was free of bees.

"Let's get out of here and find the other body," said Mary, and they headed for her car.

As they drove south, John had a chance to think. And the more he thought, the more nervous he became.

"Maybe you should drop me in town and I'll try to get a train back down to New South Wales," he said.

"Why?" asked Mary.

"Well, what am I doing here? How do we explain why I was there when we found the body?"

"When we find the body," Mary corrected him. "We haven't found it yet."

She paused. Wondering how polite she should be. Not very, she decided.

"What sort of writer are you?" she asked. "Have you ever made any money out of writing?"

"I was a reporter for nearly thirty years," John said defensively.

"Well you should know better," said Mary. "What about your books? Do they sell?"

John remained silent.

"Thought not," said Mary, "No imagination, that's your problem."

"Well I can't write this story, can I?" John almost whined, "Mike died before Rory. You'd lose everything."

"So, lie," said Mary, "Tell the story exactly as it happened except that Mike asked you to come up to Lismore to help us with the beehives. Mike and I drove down to meet you in Lismore. We drove back to Queensland and went straight on to the Daintree to set up the hives. Then Mike stayed there to settle the bees in and we drove back and found the body."

"You've been thinking about it, haven't you?" John said.

"Of course," said Mary, although in truth, she hadn't been thinking about it at all. The story had just popped into her head. What was the quotation?

'Necessity doth make liars of us all.'

As they drove up the driveway to the farmhouse and stopped in front of the shed, Mary turned to John.

"Ready?" she asked.

John nodded. Not trusting himself to speak.

Mary activated the remote and the tilt door started to

open.

Despite having seen Rory's body before, both of them gasped when they saw him again.

The interior of the shed was in semi-darkness and it looked like the body was moving.

Mary switched on the headlights. A small flock of crows were gathered around the body, pecking at it.

Mary slammed her hand on the car horn. Several of the crows flew up in alarm.

John stumbled out of the campervan and threw up on the ground.

Mary got out of the campervan, ran at the remainder of the crows, shooing them away. Having cleared the garage, Mary returned to John who was leaning on the van.

"Are you okay?" she asked, not for the first time that day. John nodded, embarrassed.

"How did they get in there?" he asked.

Mary looked at the shed. The side door was open.

"The side door," she said, "Rory must have got in that way and left it open."

Mary looked at the patch of vomit on the ground.

"Well," she said, "The police are certainly going to believe we were surprised to find the body."

They went into the house and while John was washing out his mouth, Mary rang triple O.

"What service do you require?" asked a voice.

"I'm not sure," said Mary, "A man has blown his brains out in our garage. I suppose we'll need the police, but we'll need someone to take the body away as well."

Mary gave the operator her address and what sparse details she could,

"We just arrived home and there he was. He's shot himself with a sawn-off shotgun. He's wearing a balaclava but

I think it's my brother-in-law, Rory Maguire."

"Have you touched the body?" asked the operator.

"God, no." said Mary, "He's in a pool of blood,"

Then, as an afterthought she added, "But the crows have got at him."

The words made John feel queasy again, but he managed not to throw up a second time.

When Mary hung up on the Emergency Operator she immediately dialled another number, this time on quick dial.

"Who are you calling now?" asked John.

"Mike."

"What good will that do?" John stared at her. "He's not going to answer."

"It's what I'd do if I'd really just found the body and Mike was alive," said Mary. "I'll need to include it in my statement."

Of course, the call just got a message saying the number she had just called was not available. Would she like to leave a message?

She waited for the beep then Mary said, "Mike, call me. It's important." And hung up.

John was amazed, and a bit afraid of the way Mary seemed to be thinking of everything. He'd been married several times. None of his wives could handle a spider in the bathroom.

Not that John was much better.

"I'm going for a walk," he said, "Clear my head."

"While you're there, have a look out for Rory's car," Mary said, "He usually drives a white Range Rover. If it's nowhere around, it means he must have had an accomplice."

John suddenly remembered the person with the phone

that he thought he'd seen earlier, but he decided not to mention it to Mary. He did, however, pick up a stout walking stick from the hallway stand and gripped it like a club. Mary thought this was odd, but she didn't say anything, either.

John knew the Range Rover wasn't parked in the driveway, so he set off through the rainforest, heading in the direction of the road. The first thing he found was the remains of the marijuana plantation. Roxette had made a good attempt at harvesting it. All that was left were a few stalks and off-cuts and just the occasional plant at the edge of the plantation.

She hadn't quite managed to finish the job however, nor had she had time to take the chainsaw back to the shed. It was lying among the remains of the plantation. Next to it were a set of car tracks where a vehicle had been parked while the marijuana was being loaded; and strangely, a single stocking.

John decided the chainsaw made a better potential weapon than the stick he was carrying, so he picked it up, along with the stocking, and followed the car tracks out of the rainforest and onto the road.

The tyre tracks turned left at the road and continued past the entrance to the driveway.

John followed the same route down the road until he reached the driveway. He figured Rory must have had an accomplice who had driven off with the marijuana. He was just about to return to the house when he saw something white through the trees.

Holding the chainsaw with both hands, he moved forward to investigate.

It was the Range Rover.

It was open. The keys were in the ignition. But there

was no sign of the marijuana. Whoever Rory's accomplice was had their own vehicle.

Stuffing the stocking into his pocket and still carrying the chainsaw and the walking stick, John got back to the house just before the police arrived.

Mary stared at the chainsaw.

"Where did you get that?" she asked.

"It was in the rainforest," John replied. "Were you growing marijuana?"

Mary shrugged.

"Mike was," she said, "Just for personal use. Pain control."

"He must have been in a lot of pain," said John. "There was about an acre of the stuff in there. Somebody's harvested the lot with this."

He held up the chainsaw.

"So, Rory did have someone with him," said Mary.

"I dunno," said John, "The Range Rover's still parked in the trees out there and there's no sign of the marijuana. Maybe somebody harvested it while you were down south."

"Maybe," agreed Mary, but she didn't sound convinced. And neither, really, was John. He decided to come clean.

"Look, I didn't mention it before," he said, "But I thought I saw somebody when we were here earlier. Hiding in the bush."

"And you didn't tell me?" Mary couldn't believe it.

"What could you have done? Besides, I wasn't sure. And we had to get Mike out of here."

The sound of a police siren approaching interrupted their conversation. They both stood, suddenly silent, waiting for the police car to turn into the driveway.

"Don't worry," said John, under his breath. "If whoever

it was, was involved in a plot to kill Mike, they're hardly likely to come forward. And if they harvested the marijuana, they'll be miles away from here by now."

CHAPTER TWENTY-THREE

R oxette was indeed miles away, travelling south. She had already passed through Tully and figured Townsville was probably as far south as she would get that evening. She couldn't afford to speed and get pulled over by the cops with bags of marijuana in the back of the Subaru. She intended to take her time, but she was already thinking about the problem of crossing the Queensland/ New South Wales border in the lockdown.

She used her phone to check traffic conditions on the border and got a nasty shock. The police and local Queensland town councils had been very busy since Roxette and Rory had travelled north. All roads that didn't have a police checkpoint now had concrete blocks across the road, denying access into New South Wales. She was going to need help getting the marijuana over the border.

She dialled Valerie's mobile.

Valerie answered in her usual belligerent fashion. It didn't get the conversation off to a good start.

"Where the hell have you been?" she yelled down the phone. "I haven't heard from you for over twenty-four hours."

Roxette didn't feel inclined to sugarcoat the pill.

"Rory's dead," she said, flatly. "He shot himself."

Valerie was so shocked that she had to sit down. Roxette waited for her to absorb the news.

"Why did he shoot himself?" Valerie demanded.

"You tell me," said Roxette, "You were the one he was

married to."

It occurred to Roxette that maybe that was the reason. As if reading her thoughts Valerie resumed yelling.

"It's not my fault. I wasn't there."

"Whatever," said Roxette, not wanting to get into a blame game. "Look I'm going to need help getting back across the border into New South Wales."

"Why do you need to get across the border?" Valerie asked, and if she'd left it there, no doubt Roxette would have told her about the marijuana. Instead, Valerie kept talking. "There's nothing for you here, now," she said, "If Rory's dead, Mike inherits everything. There's no Wellness Retreat, no house, no nothing. All your gold-digging has been for nothing."

Roxette wasn't offended. She didn't like Valerie anyway. Wasn't surprised or upset by her accusations. Besides, she had a car load of marijuana.

"Please yourself," she said, and hung up, already thinking of plan B.

She knew a couple of drug dealers on the Gold Coast. Roxette didn't have to cross the border to get there. She was sure they'd buy the marijuana. Even better, maybe they'd go into business with her. In these days of lockdowns and self-isolation, people had to improvise. She was sure she could persuade them to set up a home delivery service for the drugs and thereby multiply the value of the marijuana tenfold.

And when the pandemic was over and Valerie had long gone, maybe Roxette could do a deal with Mike and take over the running of the Retreat? She still had the photos and the video-recording from Mike's house. She had no idea what Mike was up to but whatever it was, she doubted he would want the police to know about it. She was sure he would be a lot more reasonable than Valerie.

As she drove sedately south, Roxette couldn't help thinking that, given the circumstances, things really hadn't worked out too badly after all.

CHAPTER TWENTY-FOUR

Mary and John were having their statements taken by the police. They had their stories down pat, but for authenticity they were conferring with each other.

"What time did we get back from down south, Mary?" asked John.

"A bit before midday, wasn't it, John?"

"About that," John nodded, "I didn't look at my watch. But we've been up to the rainforest to set up the beehives and got back here half an hour or so ago. It must have been about four hours ago or more."

The Sergeant wrote it down.

"Why didn't your husband come back with you after you'd set up the beehives?" he asked Mary.

"One of the hives doesn't have any bees in it," Mary explained. "Mike believes in catching his own bees. He's up there looking for a swarm now."

"Get the Queen in the hive," added John, "And the rest of the swarm will follow."

"Interesting," said the Sergeant and turned back to Mary "You're sure the dead man is your brother-in-law, are you?"

"As sure as I can be, given the mess the body's in," said Mary, "Perhaps you should get my husband to identify him officially. I tried phoning Mike earlier but he wasn't answering. I've left a message, but I can give you his number."

The Sergeant continued to make notes.

"And did you know your brother-in-law was coming up here?" he asked.

"No," said Mary. "The truth is my husband and his brother weren't speaking. There was a dispute over their father's will."

The Sergeant thought he smelt a motive for murder.

"So why would he come all the way up here to commit suicide?" he asked.

"Because it wasn't suicide," said an educated voice.

Everybody turned to see the Pathologist coming out of the shed, pulling down her mask.

John and Mary froze, wondering what was coming next.

The Sergeant sensed the tension.

"Not suicide?" he repeated, more convinced than ever that he might have stumbled onto a nice murder.

The Pathologist immediately quashed his hopes.

"More like death by misadventure," she said, "From the position of the body and the scratches on the freezer in there, it looks like he was trying to climb into the freezer, slipped and accidentally discharged his shotgun. The blast didn't kill him, but it knocked him backwards onto the scythe. That killed him."

"Why would he be climbing into the freezer?" The Sergeant asked, not entirely buying it.

"Maybe he was intending to lie in wait for us," said Mary, "Leap out of the freezer when we were safely inside the shed and let us have both barrels."

"Hiding in a freezer?" The Sergeant was clearly sceptical. "It'd be bloody cold, wouldn't it?"

"He wouldn't have to be there long," said John, getting into the spirit of the thing. "He just waits until the van arrives, then gets into the freezer and waits until we get out and come into the shed. Then we would've been trapped. Sitting ducks."

"That means he was getting into the freezer as you drove up," said the Sergeant, "Did you hear the gun go off?"

"No," said John, wishing he'd kept his mouth shut. Fortunately, the Pathologist inadvertently came to his aid.

"He didn't die as you drove up," she said. "Judging by the state of the body, he's been dead about four hours. Around midday."

"The time you said you first arrived," said the Sergeant suspiciously, "Did you hear a gunshot, then?"

"No," repeated John.

"Yes, we did," Mary interjected, "You remember, John? You asked what that noise was. Mike said it was probably local farmers; shooting feral pigs."

She turned to explain to the Pathologist.

"We get a lot of feral pigs up here. Play havoc with the gardens and crops."

"And you didn't go into the shed the first time you got home? After a couple of days down south?" asked the Sergeant.

"No," said Mary. "We were exhausted. We're exhausted now. Mike thought if we stopped, we'd never get going again, so we just loaded the beehive from the garden straight into the van; picked up the car because Mike was going to stay up in the Daintree, and drove on."

The Sergeant frowned.

"The car wasn't in the shed?"

"No. When we're away we keep the car parked alongside the house, so it looks like somebody's home. It's pretty isolated around here."

The Police Sergeant looked impassively at Mary. Was he

convinced?

"You've got to understand the sort of man Rory was," Mary continued. "He was struck off as a stockbroker for embezzling funds. He was up to his neck in debt; money he'd borrowed against property he doesn't own. Once the Coronavirus hit there was no way he could pay back the money he owed unless he got his hands on his father's Trust."

It sounded plausible.

The Sergeant turned to the Pathologist.

"What do you think, Doc?" he asked.

"It fits the physical evidence," said the Pathologist, "As to the fraud, the debts and the will; I guess they are all verifiable facts.

The Sergeant nodded.

"Seems open and shut, then," he said, putting away his notebook. "Can we move the body?"

"Certainly," said the Pathologist.

"Good," said the Sergeant, "Let's get this whole thing cleared up."

Despite the police being satisfied that Rory had died through misadventure, Mary was still worried.

The trouble was the pathologist. Mary had expected a middle-aged man who drank too much and missed things. Instead, the pathologist had turned out to be a sharp young woman. The way she interpreted the scene in Mary's shed was very impressive. Mary was in no doubt it was right and if she was that smart, when Mike's body was found they could be in real trouble. Especially if it hadn't thawed through completely. The pathologist was bound to spot anomalies. Mary's only hope was that Mike's body wasn't found for a long time. And that seemed unlikely.

Especially as Mike was already about to receive his first visitor.

An hour or so further north, deep in the Daintree Forest, Mike's body lay where Mary and John had dropped it. Bees buzzed around but they didn't go near the body. It was still cold and of no interest to them.

When Mary chose the site to place the beehives and Mike's body, all she was looking for was something fairly secluded; near but not visible from the river. What she hadn't noticed, and probably wouldn't have recognized if she had, was a strange groove on the riverbank, near the hives.

It looked like a slipway and that is exactly what it was. It was the place where Humphrey the crocodile came ashore to sunbathe and where afterwards he slid effortlessly back into the water. He also made the occasional foray along the bank to the camping site to check if campers had left any scraps, discarded fish or even the odd exposed limb for him to chomp on.

On this day, as usual, he emerged from the water and climbed the slipway. The newly arrived beehives didn't affect him. The bees didn't sting him and he had no taste for honey. He was also uninterested in a strange looking log across his pathway to the camping site. It was totally still, had no smell and Humphrey could feel the cold emanating from it, chilling his skin and cooling his blood. If he stayed too close for too long, he would be immobilized by the cold. He needed heat to survive. So, he ambled on into the camping site to sun himself in the clearing, and later slipped silently back into the river.

Meanwhile Mary and John were trying to decide how to proceed. Or rather, at what pace they should proceed, because they knew what they wanted to do now: claim Mike's inheritance then instruct Bob Henry to foreclose the loan on Valerie and have her evicted.

But they couldn't really get on with this until Mike's body had been found and they didn't want Mike's body found until it was properly thawed. The pathologist who had examined Rory's body had been far too smart to miss a few frozen organs when she was doing an autopsy.

Then there was the problem of Rory's possible accomplice; the person John had glimpsed, and presumably the same person who had harvested the marijuana crop. What had they seen?

John took the stocking out of his pocket and sniffed it. He explained to Mary that he'd found it near the chainsaw. It had a definite whiff of perfume; John was certain it was a woman. And she had been using the camera on her smart phone. What had she recorded? And was the woman Valerie?

Only one way to find out: ring Valerie.

So, while John got on the net to find out how long a body took to thaw, and when it would be safe for Mike's body to be found, Mary called Valerie on her mobile.

Valerie was busy filling out her application for the Job Keeper allowance that the Government was paying to small businesses that had lost more than 30% of their business and were employing people as at March 1st 2020. The Retreat certainly qualified on the first criteria. Business had gone through the floor and turnover was down to nothing. As at March 1st, the Retreat had also been employing five people: the two Thai workers who were now back in Thailand, Roxette who was in Queensland, Valerie herself, and Rory who was dead. Valerie was claiming for all of them and the farm manager and applying for nine thousand dollars per fortnight until September the 27th. She was perfectly aware that the Tax Department might catch up with the deception eventually, but by then the Retreat would be owned by Mike, so that was his problem.

In the meantime, Valerie was signing all the applications and company papers in Rory's name, so she would be in the clear. She had her story down pat.

"Should we have cancelled the Job Keeper application? Oh dear. Rory filled out the applications and he's dead. I just didn't think...."

Valerie was just practicing her lines when Mary rang.

At first Valerie thought she wouldn't respond, but then she felt an irresistible urge to abuse Mary. She picked up the phone.

"Yes?" she snapped.

Mary wasn't put off at all.

"Rory's dead," she said, flatly.

"I know," said Valerie.

Mary frowned.

"How do you know?" she asked.

Valerie cursed silently. She could hardly say Roxette had told her.

"The police told me," she snapped.

Mary was surprised. They must have been quick getting in touch with the New South Wales Police. Still, Valerie was being so snappy that Mary didn't feel like being gentle with her.

"What the hell was he doing up here with a sawn-off shotgun and wearing a balaclava?" she yelled into the phone.

"How should I know?" Valerie yelled back, even louder.

"He was up here to kill Mike, wasn't he?"

"He was not," said Valerie, "He was so upset that Mike wouldn't help him with the Trust that he shot himself. He probably wanted Mike to find his body."

"Who told you he shot himself?" asked Mary suspiciously.

Valerie realized that she had made another mistake, but she quickly covered it.

"The Police," she shouted, "Who the bloody hell do you think told me? You didn't. Your bloody husband didn't. You don't give a shit."

Mary let her rant. She knew Valerie was lying. The police knew Rory hadn't shot himself. Besides, they would have been more considerate. They would have told her there had been an accident.

"You were here with him, weren't you?" Mary said.

Valerie stopped in mid-stream.

"Of course, I wasn't," she said, sounding almost normal in her surprise. "You can check. Hang up and call me back on the landline, if you don't believe me. I'm at the farm."

Mary hung up, but she didn't bother to call back. John had been half listening as he searched the net.

"Was she here?" he asked.

"No," said Mary, "But whoever was here has been talking to her. She thought Rory had shot himself. Whoever it was must have heard the gunshot. Maybe even saw us loading Mike into the campervan."

"And filmed us with her camera," added John, ominously. "What do we do now?"

Mary poured herself a stiff drink and took a swig, and started pacing the room.

"What about me?" John asked when Mary didn't pour him a drink, or even offer him one.

"Help yourself," said Mary, "I'm thinking."

John poured himself a drink even larger than Mary's. By this time, Mary was ready for a refill. She held out her glass and John refilled it.

"What did you find on the internet?" she asked, "How long does it take for a body to defrost?"

"Well, pathologists usually defrost it over a week at a few degrees above freezing." said John, "Otherwise the outside will start to decompose while the inside is still frozen."

"It doesn't matter if the body decomposes at different speeds" said Mary, "As long as the inside is properly thawed. If it takes a week at a few degrees above freezing, it shouldn't take more than a day or two to thaw at temperatures above forty degrees, like it is up in the rainforest."

"What are you thinking?" asked John.

"We should find the body ourselves before whoever was here decides to go to the police," said Mary. " We can prove that he died from bee stings. We can say you were carrying an extra blanket to the campervan, to cover the bee hives. Nobody's going to dispute it if we show Mike died of bee stings. We've just got to get in first."

"What if the body isn't thawed right through?" asked John.

"It will be by the time the pathologist gets to it," said Mary, sounding a lot more confident than she felt.

CHAPTER TWENTY-FIVE

They decided they wouldn't drive up to the Daintree that evening. Mary wasn't even sure they could find the camp in the dark. They were both probably too drunk to drive anyway. They would wait until morning.

Mary suddenly realized that in the days since she had first discovered Mike lying dead in the bush, she had barely slept. She'd almost immediately set off for Northern New South Wales to clear his name. Then she'd visited the beehive company, the Bank and the police in quick succession and, without stopping to sleep, had driven back north with John.

By the time they had arrived at the house, both of them were ready for sleep but the shock of finding Rory dead gave her an adrenalin rush that had seen her through the ordeal of taking Mike's body to the Daintree Rainforest, and facing the subsequent interview with the police and the pathologist.

Now, Mary felt so exhausted that she didn't even dare take a bath. She thought she'd probably fall asleep and drown herself; and she couldn't rely on John to save her. She could already hear him snoring away at the far end of the house. She settled for a quick, hot shower and no sooner had her head touched the pillow than she was asleep.

A couple of hours later and she was wide awake again, staring at the ceiling fan, watching it go round and round; matching the thoughts in her head.

Originally, just four days earlier, she had decided to hide Mike's death just long enough to clear his name, then put him peacefully into the ground. Rory's attempt to murder Mike, and presumably her as well, had changed all that.

Without even thinking about it, her scheme had gone from clearing Mike's name to ensuring that Valerie didn't get her hands on the Maguire fortune; gone from a minor misdemeanour in not reporting Mike's death immediately, to a complicated fraud involving millions of dollars and the possibility of some years in goal.

How had it happened?

Well, to be honest, she felt she'd had little choice. If she'd phoned the police with Mike's body still in the freezer, she would undoubtedly have landed herself in deep trouble, and Valerie would undoubtedly have ended up with the inheritance. There was no way that was right, given that Mary was certain Valerie had been involved in the plot to kill Mike, even if Mike was already dead at the time.

No, Mary was sure she'd done the right thing. And for the right reasons. She promised herself she wouldn't touch a cent of her father-in-law's money. She would pass it on immediately to Matthew and his family; and surely, he was the one who should inherit it. The important thing now was not to tell Matthew anything. That way, should things go wrong, he couldn't be implicated.

Then Mary realized she couldn't keep everything from Matthew. If Mike had still been alive and found Rory's body, wouldn't he have phoned Matthew right away? Told him what was going on so that he wouldn't have to hear about it on the news?

Shouldn't Mary phone Matthew now? Tomorrow she

would have to call him again and tell him his father was dead. Better to split the two calls. Either one of them would be shock enough.

Mary scrabbled around for her mobile phone and called Matthew.

His voice was surprisingly alert when he answered. Working for an international company, Matthew was used to getting calls in the middle of the night. He never understood why Americans seemed unable to calculate the time difference between Australia and the States and were always calling when he was asleep.

Thinking this was another midnight business call, he had already gotten out of bed and slipped out of the bedroom to answer it without disturbing his wife when he looked at the phone and realised that the call was from his mother.

"Mum, what is it?" he asked, "Is everything all right?"

"Not really," said Mary.

"Is it dad?"

"No," said Mary, "It's your uncle Rory. Are you sitting down?"

"Yes," Matthew lied, looking behind him to make sure no lights had gone on in the bedroom and Charlotte hadn't woken up. "What about him?"

"He's dead," said Mary, "He came up to Queensland, God knows how with the border closed. He was lying in wait in our garage with a shotgun. The police think he was waiting to kill your father, but he slipped and shot himself instead."

"You're kidding!" said Matthew. "Why would he want to shoot dad?"

"For the inheritance," said Mary.

Matthew took a deep breath. Trying to take it in. Mary

filled in the silence.

"He'd committed some sort of fraud that was going to be exposed because of the Coronavirus," she explained. "With Dad dead, he would have got everything. You know about the tontine?"

"Yes," said Matthew, who was a lawyer, "You'd think grandad almost planned this when he wrote his bloody will. Is Dad okay?"

"I don't know," said Mary, "He doesn't know about Rory's death yet. He's up in the Daintree with his beehives."

"Haven't you called him?" asked Matthew.

"Of course, I've called him," said Mary. "He isn't answering his phone."

It occurred to Mary that she hadn't actually lied to Matthew. Mike didn't know about Rory's death. How could he? He was already dead himself. And he was certainly up in the Daintree with his beehives.

"I'll call him," said Matthew.

"Sure, you can try," said Mary, "I don't think you'll get an answer." (Again, not a lie) "I tried calling earlier." (ditto).

"I'll try anyway," said Matthew, "Leave a text message if nothing else. Are you all right in the house alone?"

"I'm not alone," said Mary. "Your Uncle John is with me... At least I think he's your uncle; he could be your second cousin. Anyway, he's your grandfather's nephew."

Mary realized she was babbling.

"He came up to help with Dad's beehives," she said, getting her thoughts back on track. "We're driving up to the Daintree in the morning to tell Dad what happened. I'm not looking forward to it, I can tell you."

"No, I can believe it," said Matthew, "Do you want me to

come up?"

"No," said Mary, perhaps a little too quickly, "No, you couldn't get into Queensland anyway. Not with the lock-down. You'd have to go into self-isolation. I don't suppose you could spare fourteen days up here"

"No," Matthew admitted, "Business is pretty hectic. The virus has thrown everything into chaos."

"Yes, it has," said Mary.

"Well, you take care of yourself." said Matthew, "And call me."

"I will," said Mary, "And sorry for calling you so late. I should have done it earlier."

"Yes. you should," said Matthew, not unkindly, "But as long as you and dad are okay."

Mary couldn't bring herself to reply. Instead she just hung up, wondering if she had made her situation better, or worse. It would be a lot harder calling him again, tomorrow.

She really wasn't looking forward to that.

Despite her interrupted sleep, Mary was up first. She'd showered and was cooking breakfast but there was still no sign of John.

It was a typical Far North Queensland day. What was the saying? *'Beautiful one day, perfect the next.'* It was certainly a prefect day for thawing a body. The sun was barely up but already the temperature was into the forties. Mike's body would be baking in the sun. Mary felt she really ought to have protected it. Sunburn over the bee stings would only complicate matters. Still, too late now.

She went into the kid's bedroom where John was curled up in a ball, clinging precariously to the single bed as if he was afraid that he'd fall out.

Mary was pretty sure he was feigning sleep. She gave

him a swift punch anyway.

"Come on, get up.'

John sat up and pulled the sheets closer to him. Mary suspected he slept in the nude but she wasn't concerned with such niceties.

"Come on," she said, "Breakfast is cooking."

John didn't move.

"Perhaps you should go on your own," he said.

"No way," said Mary, "I thought you wanted to write the book."

John had been thinking about that as he lay in bed feigning sleep.

"Well I can't write it now, can I?" he said. "God knows what laws we've broken and crimes we've committed."

"I don't believe in God, said Mary, "And nobody else knows."

"The woman with the camera knows," said John.

"She hasn't come forward, has she?" said Mary, "Why not? Probably because she's got the marijuana. She's too busy selling it. Let's find Mike before she does. Move yourself. Breakfast's ready in five minutes."

Mary exited to the kitchen but John still didn't move. He was thinking it through. Could he write the story and still remain in the clear? He eventually decided he could. He could even include the marijuana. Everything would be the same except that it would have been Mike and Mary who had taken the beehives up to the Rainforest. It would be a great story. Two feuding brothers: one a fraudster; the other a drug dealer. A story of justice being done, though neither was blameless.

He decided not to mention this new version of the book to Mary. Instead he headed to the bathroom for a shower. The sooner they found the body, the sooner he could disappear back down south and leave everything to her.

Clear now about what his book would be, John again reverted to reporter mode as they drove up to the Daintree. He asked Mary about the trolling. What the reaction had been? He clucked and sounded sympathetic. Mary wondered what he was up to, then decided he was just nervous and needed to think about something other than finding Mike's body and calling the police. So, she told him everything about herself and Mike, although she was a little wary when he kept harping on about the marijuana plantation, asking if Mike might have been a dealer.

When they finally drove into the camp site, Mary switched off the ignition and sat there for a moment. She wasn't sure whether she just didn't want to leave the cool of the air-conditioned car, or whether she was afraid of what she would see when they found Mike's decomposing body. He had looked terrible when she had first found him with the bee stings. Now he could only look worse.

John didn't let her prevaricate.

"Come on," he said, "Let's get it over with."

He got out of the car and started yelling, "Mike! Mike!"

Alarmed, Mary scrambled out of the car after him.

"What are you doing?"

"Calling Mike," said John, "That's what we'd do if we drove into his camp and he didn't come to greet us. Maybe there's somebody around. If they hear us, it'll sound natural."

Mary was certain John was overthinking the thing.

"Let's get it over with," she said, and set off towards the beehives.

Insects still buzzed around everywhere and she had to swot them away. She'd forgotten to bring any insect repellent. A bad move. God knows what insects would be swarming around Mike's body. She knew that he would have insect repellent in the campervan but she couldn't turn back. John had forged ahead and he'd already reached the spot where they'd left Mike's body. He was staring around, looking confused. Mary wondered who he was play-acting for now? When she reached him, she realized he wasn't acting at all.

There was no body there.

"Isn't this where he was?" John asked.

"Yes," agreed Mary.

"Oh shit," said John, "Somebody must have found him."

"I don't think so," said Mary, looking at the marks on the ground. She walked towards the river. One of Mike's wellington boots was lying on the ground. Mary picked it up, stared ahead to the riverbank. The slipway that Humphrey used was clearly visible, now that she was looking more closely.

She turned to John, "I think a crocodile's taken him," she said.

"Oh, thank Christ for that," said John.

Mary stared at him.

"What are you saying?"

John shrugged, apologetically.

"Well, it's better than somebody else finding him still half thawed," he said, but he was thinking: *'A crocodile! Shit! What a great chapter for the book.'*

Out loud, he said,

"Shall I phone the cops, or will you?"

He pulled his mobile out of his pocket.

"Hold it," said Mary. She was desperately trying to compute the ramifications of what had happened.

"We can't call the police," she said, "If Mike's disappeared, we have no proof he's dead or when he died. We won't be able to do anything with his father's will. Valerie will hang on to everything like grim death. She might even claim the crocodile could have taken him before we arrived back at the house and found Rory. Nobody's seen Mike since we found Rory's body."

"What about the woman with the camera?"

"She probably thinks you're Mike," Mary agreed, "But we can hardly call her as a witness."

"Well, what are we going to do?" Mike asked, his flair for writing deserting him. Original plot was never his strongpoint. He was more of a reporter.

"Obviously Mike can't die," said Mary, after some thought. "At least, not yet."

"But he is dead," said John, "The crocodile's got him."

"Nobody knows that, except you and me. You'll have to pretend to be Mike for a little while longer."

"No way," said John.

"If you don't," said Mary, "If Valerie gets the Trust, I'll have nothing more to lose. I'll tell everybody the truth. Everything. Right back to the blood tests and the horses at the abattoir."

John knew he was trapped.

"How long is this going on?" he whined.

"Just until the Trust's settled," Mary said, "Then I'll discover that Mike's been taken by a crocodile."

"I'm not coming back here," said John.

"You don't have to. I'll drive the campervan back up here, put Mike's hat, gloves and boot and phone back down here, then I'll ride home on Mike's trailbike."

She began collecting these items, while John just stood there, still whinging.

"What if Mike's body turns up in the meantime?"

"It's not likely to," said Mary, "With the lockdown, there

are no tourists, and there won't be for a while. Besides," she added, "If anyone does find it, it isn't likely to be in one piece. It'll be unrecognizable."

But in fact Mike's body was still in one piece. Crocodiles only eat about once a week and Humphrey hadn't taken Mike's body because he was hungry. He'd taken it because it was there.

As usual he'd returned to his sunbathing spot earlier that morning to warm himself before the sun got too high and too hot and he would have to retreat to the shade. He had smelt Mike long before he saw him. He could smell him even before he emerged from the river. The smell had been so enticing, he made a beeline for the body.

Being a pre-historic reptile with a very small brain, it didn't occur to Humphrey that this sweet-smelling delicacy was the same block of ice he'd encountered the previous evening and sought to avoid. Now it was warm and soft, at least on the outside.

Humphrey crept up on the body and lunged, grabbing it by the head, which he practically swallowed. He threw himself into a death roll. Mike's neck broke. His arms and legs flayed in the air, throwing off both his wellington boots; one of which landed on the ground nearby, while the other was hurled into the water and sailed silently down the river.

Convinced that his prey was now dead, or at least incapacitated, Humphrey pulled him backwards into the water. Once submerged, he did a second and third death roll to ensure that Mike was dead, then he carried the carcass in his mouth, downstream to where the mangrove swamps bordered the river.

The mangrove swamps were Humphrey's larder. He

kept his bigger prey, anything larger than a single meal, trapped in the roots of the mangroves, below the low water mark.

The carcass would remain there for several weeks, because even when he started to eat it, it was more than a single meal. Provided the smaller pieces of the carcass didn't float away as Humphrey was pulling it apart to eat, it would provide him with food for a month. Again provided, of course, that any other crocodile, or even an alert Forest Ranger, didn't happen upon his larder.

CHAPTER TWENTY-SIX

A s they travelled south, back towards Mary's place, John drove the campervan, following Mary in her car. Mary thought it would look better if anybody saw them. Everybody knew that the campervan belonged to Mike; the little hatchback belonged to her.

Mary used her driving time to plan her next move.

She knew what she wanted. To clear Mike's name and to thwart Valerie. To do this, the first thing was to prove that Mike was alive after Rory had died.

Which led her to the thought; in a time of Covid and isolation, how do we know if anybody is still alive? Well, obviously you talk to them. How? By email, Facebook and other social media, video conferencing, but firstly by phone.

Shit. Mary had forgotten that.

Not surprisingly, Mike hadn't used his phone since he'd died. If there was ever a query about when he died, the first thing the police would check would be his phone records.

Ignoring the dangers inherent in taking her hand off the steering wheel and her eyes off the road, Mary scrambled about in her bag and brought out Mike's phone. She found her phone charger and plugged it into the cigarette lighter plug. She waited a few minutes before phoning John.

In the campervan, John looked at his phone. Mike was phoning him. What the hell was going on? Then he realized it must be Mary. Using his hands free, he answered the call.

"Hello?"

"We should have been using Mike's phone," said Mary.

"We thought he was dead," said John.

"Well, now we think he isn't, we should use it. You should use it to call the executor of the estate when we get back home."

John didn't like the sound of that.

"And tell him what?" he asked.

"Tell him that Rory's dead and to send up whatever papers you need to sign to claim the Trust."

"Now you want me to forge documents," John exclaimed, feeling the whole thing was spiralling out of control.

"And tell him to foreclose on Valerie for the house and the Retreat and kick her out," said Mary, ignoring his objections.

"Isn't that a bit harsh?" asked John, fearing that the harder they were on Valerie, the harder she would fight to keep the property.

"Her husband tried to kill Mike," said Mary, "She must have been in on it. I'll tell you what, set up a video call with the executor and her. I'd love to see her face when she learns that she's losing everything. Not that she probably doesn't realise that already."

John was still reluctant.

"I'm not sure I can pull this off," he said, "What if they realise that I'm not Mike?"

"They won't. It won't even occur to them"

"What if they ask questions I can't answer?"

"I'll sit behind the screen, out of sight, and write down the answers to anything you don't know."

John thought he saw a flaw in Mary's argument.

"If she can't see you on the screen, you can't see her," he said.

Mary had thought of that.

"We'll record the conference call on Mike's phone," she said. "We'll need a record of the call anyway."

Calling Bob Henry with Mike's phone on speaker was the easy part. Bob hadn't heard that Rory was dead so he said he couldn't execute the will until he had proof.

"Phone the local cops here," said John, "Or I'll phone them. Believe me, he's dead."

"It's not that I don't believe you," said Bob, who wasn't at all happy about handing Mike's inheritance over to him and doing himself out of a job as the executor in the process; particularly in the middle of an expensive divorce. "But things have to be done by the book."

Mary scribbled furiously on a piece of paper which she held up to John.

"Really?" he read into the phone, "In that case how come you loaned Rory Trust money to buy the farmhouse and the Retreat? You were lending him my money to buy property we owned. Is that by the book?"

Mary wished this call was on video. She would have loved to see Bob squirm. He was always such an officious little sod, acting as if he owned the Trust.

"I thought it was a good investment," Bob was muttering as Mary scribbled another message.

While he waited for Mary's prompt, John was getting into the spirit of the thing.

"Well you were wrong, weren't you?" he said.

"Nobody could have foreseen the virus," Bob protested.

"It wasn't best business practice, virus or no virus," John snapped, before reading what Mary was holding up,

"Look, I don't want to waste any more time. Arrange a video call with Valerie and me tomorrow. I'll tell the pair of you what's happening at the same time. Say ten o'clock."

John switched off the phone before Bob Henry could respond.

"Very good," said Mary, clapping her hands. John grinned. He was beginning to enjoy the play-acting. Especially since he knew that when he wrote the book, it would be Mike playing the bastard; not him.

While Mary prepared dinner, John sat with his notes, going over everything he knew about Mike, Rory, their father and their father's will.

"He was a right bastard, your father-in-law, wasn't he?" John said.

"Yes," said Mary. "And Rory inherited his nature. Not like Mike. He was always too soft."

"Really?" said John, "Maybe I shouldn't have gone so hard with the executor?"

"No," said Mary, "Go as hard as you like. I'm sure having your brother try to kill you would toughen up even the mildest person."

John made a note of that. It would go down well in the book.

The following morning, as ten o'clock approached, Mary arranged a place for John to sit with his back to the sliding glass doors which opened out on to the verandah, so that he was backlit. His face was still visible but in shadow and he was wearing Mike's clothes. His hair was cut and combed the way Mike wore his hair. John was still a little nervous that Valerie might realise that he wasn't Mike, but Mary reassured him by telling him that on one occasion Mike had grown a beard when they went up to visit Rory and Valerie. They were there for a week before either of them even noticed the beard. And then it was only because Mike had pointed it out to them.

Satisfied with John's position, Mary positioned herself behind the computer screen with a chalkboard that she normally used in her Grade One classes. Even in the half-light John could easily read anything written on it.

Bob Henry hosted the video conference and he and Valerie were already visible on the screen when John logged in. Bob was trying to sound as impartial and as friendly as he could manage, but it was a lost cause.

Firstly, John told him that he was recording the whole conversation on his phone, and he held up Mike's phone and pointed it at the screen, to prove it.

"I've no objections," said Bob.

Valerie shrugged.

"Neither have I," she said. "I don't even know why I was included in this call."

"You will," said John, "You will.'

Valerie scowled while Bob tried to keep things at least civilized, if not friendly.

"First of all, Valerie," he said, "I'd like to say how sorry I was to hear of Rory's death."

"Humpph," came from Valerie, "'Course you are, because it means you have to hand the Trust over to Mike. No more chances to fiddle the books and siphon off your share."

"I have always acted honourably," said Bob in an offended tone.

"What about the loans for the farmhouse and the Retreat?" asked John.

"I've explained all that," Bob snapped, no longer making any pretence of politeness.

"Yeah, well," said John, "Now you can put it right. How soon can you foreclose on both loans?"

"You can't do that," Valerie yelled. "Rory's not even in the ground, yet. Have some respect!"

"Respect," John yelled back, "Your bloody husband tried to kill me."

"Nonsense," insisted Valerie, making a very good stab at pretending to sob. "If he was trying to kill you, why would he have killed himself? It's all your fault. If you'd agreed to split the Trust, Rory would never have been in trouble. You drove him to it. You killed him. You drove him to shoot himself."

Mary was scribbling furiously but she needn't have bothered. John knew exactly what to say.

"He didn't shoot himself," he said, "He slipped and fell on a scythe while he was trying to hide in the freezer so he could jump out and shoot me. The scythe practically cut his head off. If fact, if you want, the undertakers could send you down his head and body in separate caskets."

Valerie's tears disappeared immediately.

"What are you talking about?"

"Oh, you mean "the Police" didn't tell you?" said John, his voice dripping with sarcasm. "He was trying to ambush us when he tripped and fell. Don't take my word for it, ask the Queensland Police. No doubt they'll be talking to you, anyway. Asking what your husband was doing in our shed with a sawn-off shot-gun, wearing a balaclava? Don't suppose there's any chance your fingerprints might be on the shot-gun as well?"

Valerie had a sudden flashback of herself handing Rory the shot-gun, but she covered it well.

"I don't know anything about it," she said, "He just

disappeared with his tart, Roxette. He didn't even tell me where he was going."

Roxette is an unusual name. Mention of it sparked a memory from John's notes.

"Would that be Roxette Simpson?" he asked. "The one who's been accusing Mi…" John quickly corrected himself, "My wife and me of being paedophiles?"

"I don't know," said Valerie, not noticing John's slip of the tongue, "I don't know what they've been up to."

"It must have been terrible for you," said John, as if he believed her. "I bet you can't wait to put it all behind you. Leave that terrible place. Well , I can help you there. Mr. Henry, foreclose on that loan as soon as it's legal."

"You've forgotten something," said Valerie. "The Bank has given me a six month's moratorium on repayments because of the Covid virus."

Behind the screen, Mary was shocked. John didn't even miss a beat.

"And Mr. Henry," he continued, "Inform the Bank, the *Head Office* of the Bank, that we're foreclosing. I doubt they'll be granting any moratorium when they realise they can't get their money back."

Valerie didn't respond; her screen just went dark. She had logged out. Bob Henry was staring at John on the screen and shaking his head.

"Any problems?" John asked him.

"No," said Bob Henry, "It's just that I always thought Rory took after his old man. I thought he was the bastard. I thought you were the soft one. But you're worse than both of them."

"Yeah, well, having your brother try to kill you, will do that to you, every time," said John, finding the perfect place in the book for Mike to make that statement.

The only thing left for Mary and John to do was to wait until the papers came up from the Trust's solicitor. Mary insisted that John wait and take the papers to a local solicitor to sign. More proof that Mike was alive. Once that was done John could return to Sydney and Mary could return Mike's belongings to the Daintree.

The Coronavirus seemed to have passed its peak, in Queensland at least, and things were beginning to open up again. This was a two-edged sword.

On the one hand it meant John could travel back to New South Wales and resume his life; and Mary could then leave the campervan and Mike's wellington boot and bee-keeper gear up in the Daintree, so that he could resume his death.

On the other hand, with society opening up again and people being allowed to visit National Parks within fifty kilometres of their homes, it meant there would be more people in the Daintree Rainforest and therefore more chance that someone might find the remains of Mike's body. But since the Daintree National Park covered more than twelve hundred square kilometres and had only about one thousand inhabitants, the chances of this happening were still pretty slim.

In the meantime, John made himself useful.

The first thing he did was visit the Principal at Mary's school. Fearing he was getting a bit over-confident, Mary suggested he just put in a conference call to the school, but John insisted on seeing the Principal face to face. Mary decided she had better go along too, to stop John from making a fool of himself.

She needn't have worried. John wasn't channelling Mike. He was more like Rory; finding a devious way around everything.

"You realise that you are making my wife's life a living hell?" was his opening remark to the Principal.

It was hard to tell who was the more shocked, the Principal or Mary.

The Principal floundered, while Mary tried to keep a straight face.

"I don't know what you mean," said the Principal.

"Yes, you do," said John, "This social media campaign against me. You obviously believed it. The least you could have done was talk to me, or talk to the New South Wales Education Department."

He produced a sheaf of emails and banged them on the desk.

"They could have told you that there never was a pupil named Roxette Simpson at my school in Sydney. They could have sent you the inquiry papers on the other accusations. The record of my complete exoneration. Instead you practically barred my wife from teaching."

"Oh no," said the Principal, "Oh no, we never did."

She turned to Mary.

"You must have misunderstood me, Mrs. Maguire. The school's about to re-open. You are, of course, more than welcome to come back and resume face-to-face teaching. That is, if you don't think your age will put you at any particular risk," she added, considerately.

"I beg your pardon?" said Mary, feeling almost as outraged by the suggestion that she was too old, as she had been by the suggestion that she had turned a blind eye to her husband's paedophilia.

" I just mean...it's your decision, entirely, Mrs. Maguire," the Principal went on hurriedly.

"That's settled then," said John, "And if you want to know anything more about me, you only have to ask."

He stood up.

"Let's go Mary."

John was already heading for the door. Mary stood, paused,

"You'll have to forgive him," she almost whispered to the Principal. "His brother has just died in a terrible accident."

The Principal nodded, and whispered back,

"Yes, of course, I understand. We'll see you tomorrow then, Mrs. Maguire."

Mary didn't catch up with John until he was crossing the playground. Even then they didn't speak. They didn't make a sound until they were safely seated in Mary's car. Then they both burst out laughing.

"Did you see her face when I said she'd made your life a living hell?" asked John.

"Well, it's true," said Mary, stifling her laughter, "but you missed the best bit when I told her you had just lost your brother in a terrible accident. She tried so hard to look sympathetic."

Eventually they stopped laughing.

"Well," said John, "What next?"

"We're going to get Mike's Queensland driving licence," said Mary, "With your photograph on it, nobody is ever going to doubt that you are Mike."

Both Mary and John decided to try to stay busy until the

solicitor's papers arrived.

Mary resumed teaching and was overjoyed to be back with her little Grade Ones. The Principal had been as good as her word and told everyone that the claims that Mike was a paedophile were nonsense, so Mary was once again popular with staff, parents and students.

John spent his time at the house, writing his book, and as always when he was writing, he did almost anything rather than actually sit down and write. He made cups of tea. He prepared the evening meal. He cleaned the bathrooms. Eventually he took the chainsaw and cut down the last of the marijuana plants.

He put the remaining leaves and seeds into small cellophane bags and hung them up in the shed to dry, and he roughly mulched the remains of the stalks of the plants and distributed them around the forest floor.

Chopping up the marijuana released its terpenes and hence its aroma. Breathing in the fumes for a few hours while he worked in the forest made John feel quite lightheaded and relaxed; the perfect state to actually sit down and do some writing. So, while he munched away on potato chips, sandwiches and just about anything else he could find, he made big inroads into writing the book.

He started with Mike's father being shipped to Australia. The things that made him tough, the things that made him heartless, and the relationship between Rory and Mike, before and after their father's will had set them up as rivals.

At that point he came up with his first title: *Family Feud.*

It had the advantage of being both familiar and appropriate and while everybody knew the TV Program, he was pretty sure there wasn't a book of that name. He went off to raid the pantry to find more food, thinking that the title was a work of genius.

When Mary came home, John was still at the computer, although he had put a curry on to cook and made some dahl. Mary just had to boil the rice.

As she prepared the rice she asked, "What are those bags hanging in the garage?

"Ah, just the remains of the marijuana crop." he said, "For medicinal purposes only," he added, remembering the excuse Mike had given Mary for growing marijuana in the first place.

Mary had put up with it from Mike. She wasn't putting up with it from John.

"I don't want that stuff in my house," she said.

"Don't worry," said John, "I'll be taking it south with me, when I go. It'll only be there a couple of days."

"Make sure you do," said Mary.

John used Mary's arrival home as an excuse to stop working and pour them each a glass of wine.

"How was your day?" he asked.

"Really good," she said, "the kids were so excited to be back at school. They all washed their hands with great enthusiasm, but getting them to socially distance was a bloody impossibility. They'll be all right. We haven't had a new Covid case in Queensland for a week now."

"The virus and the isolating seem to have just passed us by," said John, "It'll be a bit lonely up here when I'm gone."

"You're not staying," said Mary, perhaps a little too quickly.

"No, no," John said, "Never intended to. But you will call me? Let me know how it goes when you eventually report Mike missing?"

"Of course," said Mary, "And you will send me a copy of your manuscript before you give it to your publisher?"

"Of course," said John, "I'm thinking of calling it *'Family Feud'*."

"Umm, nice," said Mary. "Familiar but accurate."

"That's what I thought," said John, and they were both sipping their wine and thinking how clever they'd been when a police car appeared in the driveway.

"Oh shit!" said Mary, putting down her glass and picking up her car keys with the shed door remote on it. She made a dash through the house to the shed.

As the police car pulled up outside, John decided to bluff it out and go to talk to them. If nothing else it would distract them from Mary closing the shed door to prevent them seeing the marijuana.

John stepped out onto the balcony, still holding his glass of wine.

"Gentlemen," he said to the two young cops getting out of the car, "What can I do you for?"

A gag neither of the young cops paid any attention to.

"Michael Maguire?" said the older of the policemen who John thought looked about nineteen.

"Yes," said John "Is there anything wrong?"

Mary stepped out from inside the house just in time to hear the policeman say,

"It's about your brother."

"What about him?" John asked, stiffening.

"Well, it's a bit embarrassing really," said the policeman, "We've been in touch with his wife."

"What about her?" asked John, feeling increasingly nervous.

"We told her we could now release his body. She said we could do what we liked with it. Feed it to the crocodiles, if we wanted to."

John looked at Mary, not sure what to say.

"We'll take care of it, of course," Mary broke in. "After all he is family. Even if he did try to kill us. With Covid we can't have a memorial service, but we'll lay him to rest."

"Wouldn't he rather be cremated?" asked John, thinking that if he was incinerated and they did find Mike's body, there would be no chance to check his DNA.

Whether Mary thought of that or not, she agreed, "Very suitable," she said, "Consign him to the fires of hell."

Not sure whether Mary was joking or not, the police officers gave John the name of the local undertaker that they usually used and headed back for their car.

"Doubt if they'd have bothered about a few marijuana plants in the garage, anyway," said John.

"That's what Mike always said. I just don't want the cops hanging around here for any reason at all at the moment," said Mary. "I'll chase up the solicitors; make sure they've emailed up those papers. You can sign them tomorrow and be on your way."

"No way," said John, "I've got to be at the cremation. It'll be one of the highlights of the book. Besides, isn't that what Mike would have done?"

"Yes," smiled Mary, "And he'd probably have read the eulogy."

CHAPTER TWENTY-EIGHT

A couple of days later and John was heading back to Sydney at last, happy not to have to keep pretending he was Mike. His last act in that regard was to attend Rory's cremation. Nothing much happened there that would make particularly good reading in the book but John did observe, wryly, that apart from the undertaker and the crematorium attendant, the only people there were Mary and himself; or as it would say in the book, Mary and Mike. It was ironic that the only mourners at Rory's funeral were his two intended victims, John noted in his book.

After the service Mary was keen to get John back to Sydney as soon as possible. The problem was, how? Because of the travel restrictions still in place, there were no available flights. There was a daily train from Cairns to Brisbane, but that was only for essential travellers and it would be hard for John to explain that it was essential he get out of town so that Mary could replace the evidence on the riverbank in the Daintree to prove that Mike had been taken by a crocodile.

Then they remembered Rory's Range Rover, still sitting amongst the trees near the property entrance. They checked with Bob Henry and discovered, as they thought, that the Range Rover belonged to the farm, not to Rory personally, and therefore now belonged to Mike.

Mary had ordered Bob Henry to re-hire Dave, the farm manager that Rory had sacked when the Covid virus first hit. He was already working, preparing the farm for the harvest. John would drive the Range Rover south but because he didn't want to bump into Valerie at the farm, and because he had to pick up his own car from the motel carpark in Lismore, he arranged to meet Dave the motel.

As John drove into the carpark, Dave was already waiting with Darren, a casual labourer who would be helping with the harvest and would now drive Dave's truck back to the farm.

Dave greeted John like a long-lost friend.

"G'day Mike," he said, "How's the grandkid? Haven't seen him up on the farm for years."

John had been pretending to be Mike for so long, he didn't know whether to continue the subterfuge or not. He quickly decided not. Mike's body might be found soon. He didn't want Dave wondering how he could be in two places at once.

"Actually, you're mistaking me for my cousin," he said. "I'm John. I'm Mike's cousin."

Dave almost did a double take.

"Shit. You're the spitting image.."

"People do say that," agreed John.

Dave introduced Darren.

"This is Darren," he said, "He's working on the harvest. Do you want to see the farm? It's a bit of a mess. Been left alone when there was pruning and cleaning up to be done."

"No, I won't bother," said John, eager to just get away. "If you've got any problems with anything," he continued, "Just let Mike know up in Cairns. Otherwise he'll be leaving it pretty much to you."

"That's what Rory used to do," said Dave, "Lazy bastard."

He grinned to indicate that he was joking; although he

wasn't.

"You'll probably be saying the same about Mike," said John.

"Yeah, but he won't be pretending he's the manager, will he?" said Dave.

"No, no, you probably won't even be seeing him," said John, "Although when Valerie moves out, no doubt Matthew and his family will be spending more time up here."

"She's moved out," said Dave, "Just shot through without telling anybody. The guru, or shaman or whatever she is, Daintree, she's still living in the Retreat, but."

"Don't know her," said John.

"No," agreed Dave, "She's only been there a few months."

John nodded.

"Well," he said, "I've got to be off"

Dave nodded, held out his hand.

"Tell young Mattie and the family to come up anytime," he said, "I'll drive 'em around on the tractor. Make 'em into farmers in no time."

Ignoring Covid protocols, they all shook hands and Dave and Darren got into their respective vehicles and drove off.

John gave a sigh of relief. Happy that didn't have to pretend he was Mike anymore. Happy that he could soon finish the book and get it to his publisher.

He picked up his suitcase and the black bin liner from Mary's garage that he'd filled with marijuana, and headed for his car. Dumping the bin liner and the suitcase into his boot, he got into the car with a sigh, and switched on the ignition.

Nothing.

In the time he'd been away, his battery had gone flat.

He'd have to call the NRMA Road Service. Trouble was, he wasn't a member and he'd have to join. Still it would be worth it to get back to Sydney, get back to his own life and finish the book. Then as soon as Mary called to tell him a crocodile had taken Mike, he could publish it.

Mary had waited a day or so after John drove off, to give him time to get back into New South Wales, then she headed back up to the Daintree. She had Mike's phone, one Wellington boot, a beekeeper's hat and gloves, and the bee-smoker; all of which she put into a bin liner and stowed in the campervan.

She had also put Mike's trailbike and helmet into the van. She had been practicing riding the bike around the property and through the bush where the marijuana plantation had once been. She didn't have a motorbike license, but she judged that she was proficient enough to ride the bike home, although she'd taken the added precaution of getting a set of 'L' plates, just in case the police saw her riding along and thought she looked a bit unsafe.

As it turned out she didn't pass a single vehicle all the way up to the Daintree and she hoped it would be equally quiet on the way home.

She drove into the clearing where Mike usually parked the campervan, grabbed the bin liner and headed for the beehives. Her plan was to get in and out as quickly as possible, so that nobody would know she was there without Mike.

She walked through the trees beside the river until she came to the spot where they'd left the bee hives. At least she thought it was the spot; but there was no sign of the hives.

She looked at the river. The crocodile slipway into the river was clearly visible. This was the right spot. Somebody had moved the bee hives.

She looked around frantically, and then froze as she heard a voice behind her.

"G'day, where's Mike?"

Mary turned. It was Warren, the Park Ranger, grinning at her, showing a set of perfect, white teeth.

"He's out in the bush," said Mary, not even needing time to think up the lie. "He's gone bush, looking for swarms of bees. He's already caught one lot that he's got in a hive up here. He asked me to check on it, but I can't find it."

"I moved them," said Warren.

"Why?"

Warren pointed to the slipway on the riverbank.

"See that?"

Mary stared at the riverbank as if she'd never seen the slipway before.

"It's a crocodile slipway," explained Warren. "A big bull. Name's Humphrey. He comes up here and suns himself. If Mike was working on his hives, he might have got taken."

"My God!" said Mary, doing her best to sound like a dumbstruck teenager. "You give the crocodiles names?"

"Only the big ones," said Warren, "Come on, I'll show you where I've put the hives."

They walked back to the campsite and on into the bush.

The bee hives stood in dappled sunlight a little way from the river.

"I don't suppose crocodiles would ever come this far from the river?" said Mary, hoping to be contradicted.

"Oh, they'd come this far," said Warren, "In flood, the river comes this far. You get water up to here."

He pointed at the ground. Near the bank it was brown and fairly bare.

"See where the vegetation has been washed away in the

floods? But the hives should be okay."

He scratched the three-day growth on his chin.

"I noticed only one of 'ems got bees in..."

"Yes," said Mary. "Mike's hoping to find another swarm."

"There's a nest nearby," said Warren. "If you want to give me a hand, we could catch the Queen. Give Mike a surprise when he comes up, next time."

"Oh," said Mary. "Um..okay".

She wasn't sure if it was a such good idea but couldn't think of a reason to say no.

"What's in the bag?" Warren asked.

"Oh, a hat and gloves and a smoker," said Mary.

"Well you wear 'em," said Warren, "I'll be right. Been doing this since I was a nipper. I'll have the smoker, but."

He took the bin liner from Mary and looked inside.

"There's a wellington boot in 'ere as well," he said.

"Is there? Only one? God, I'm stupid. Must have left the other one at home." said Mary, hoping desperately that Warren hadn't found the other one floating down the river.

Back at the motel carpark in Lismore, John was still waiting for the NRMA when a Subaru with some sort of insignia on the side, beeped its horn, drove into the carpark and stopped near him. The insignia on the side was a snake wrapped around a staff; the staff of Asclepios, the symbol for medicine.

John was surprised. He knew that in a lot of small towns the NRMA didn't have regular road service assist vans. They used the local garage as a stringer, but he'd never heard of them using a doctor.

He was even more surprised when the driver got out of the car and said,

"Hello, Mike."

She was an attractive blonde in what looked like a doctor's coat.

John just frowned.

"It's Roxette," said the woman, "You saw me up in Cairns. Remember?" and she mimed using her phone as a camera to take his picture.

John recognised the allusion with a shock.

"You were with Rory!" he blurted out, "You tried to kill..."

He hesitated briefly. Should he say Mike or should he say me? Should he be Mike or should he be John? In the end he settled for,

"... us. You tried to kill us!"

Roxette didn't seem to notice the hesitation.

"No," she said, "Rory told me that he was going to rob a bank. I was as surprised as you. Especially when he shot himself."

"I don't suppose you thought of going to the police?" said John.

"Nooo," Roxette repeated, "Why would I? Especially with a carload of marijuana. But I saw you clearing the drugs out of the shed before you guys called the police. You're a naughty boy."

Obviously Roxette thought Mike's blanket-wrapped body was drugs. Despite the relief John felt on hearing this, he still felt compelled to deny everything.

"I don't know what you're talking about."

"It's okay," Roxette soothed, "You did me a favour. Set me up in a nice little business during the Covid shutdown." Roxette gestured to her car, "Home deliveries: marijuana. For medicinal purposes only, of course."

She moved closer to John.

"You know what? We should go into business together. I'll run the Retreat for you and we'll start another little plantation in the rainforest on the farm."

"I don't think so," said John, shaking his head.

"Or," Roxette continued as if he hadn't spoken, "I can send the pictures of you and Mary carrying the dope out of the garage, and of Rory's body in the shed, to the Police. Anonymously, of course."

Roxette placed a familiar hand onto John's chest.

"Come on, Mike. I'll do all the work. We'll split the profits, 50/50. We'll make a fortune."

John knew he was trapped. At least until he was far away from Northern New South Wales and Mike's disappearance was reported in Queensland.

"Tell you what," he said, "I've got another bin liner full of hooch in the car. Enough to keep you going until I get back."

Roxette smiled.

"You're so much nicer than your brother," she said.

Warren's technique for capturing a Queen bee was considerably more efficient than Mike's efforts to knock a swarm of bees off a branch and into a box.

Warren wrapped the bin liner completely around the bees' nest, broke the top of the nest from the tree, closed the bin liner over the nest and tied the top.

He was just carrying the bin liner full of bees to the free-flow hive when Mary's phone rang.

It was John.

Mary was wondering whether to answer it when Warren said,

"You answer it. I can manage here."

Mary swiped the phone, turned her back on Warren and spoke before John had a chance to say anything.

"Mike! Hi darling," she said, "You are a stupid boy. I'm up here in the Daintree with Warren Hodgson. He says the place you put the hives was right next to the favourite haunt of a huge crocodile. He reckons you could have been taken if you weren't careful."

John realized there was someone there with Mary, but who?

"Who the hell's Warren Hodgson?" he asked.

Mary seemed to ignore him.

"Of course, being a *park ranger*, Warren knows all about the local crocs and bees," she said, "He's moved your hives and he's even helping me stock the free-flow hive with a Queen."

"Are you all right?" John asked.

"Yes," said Mary, and continued without hesitating, "He says crocodiles could come ashore, even where he's put the hives now, but not until the rainy season. You'll have to be careful then."

"When is the rainy season?" John asked.

"Oh, months away," Mary said airily, as if it didn't matter that they couldn't stage Mike's disappearance for months.

"That could be a problem, said John, "I met Roxette. She's the woman on the website of the Golden Topaz Retreat. She calls herself Daintree Simpson there. She wants to go into business with us, running the Retreat and growing marijuana in the farm's rainforest."

"No way!" said Mary, so adamantly that she had to smile reassuringly as Warren looked at her with alarm.

"I don't think we have any choice," said John, "She was the one with Rory at the house. The one who took the marijuana. The one with the camera when we were putting Mike in the camper; although she thinks it was you and

Mike hiding drugs."

"All done," said Warren, and stood back to admire his handiwork.

He had obviously succeeded in getting the Queen into the free-flow hive; all the rest of the bees were buzzing around it. Warren had been stung a couple of times but it didn't seem to affect him.

"Warren, you're a marvel," Mary said, and watched as Warren took a large knife from his belt; not a Crocodile Dundee large knife, but a large knife nonetheless.

He scraped the sharp edge of the blade along his skin over a bee stinger which was still protruding from the skin. The stinger came out, poison and all. Warren merely flipped the knife, flicking the stinger off the blade, then moved on to the next sting.

Such a simple action.

Mary wondered, if Mike had known about it would it have saved his life? The thought brought tears to her eyes and she had to turn away as she spoke into the phone.

"Darling, Warren's got the Queen into the free- flow hive. We'll be having our own honey by the time you come back up here."

"I'm not coming back up there," said John.

"Of course not," said Mary, "You stay right where you are. Maybe you could start dinner when you've finished? Oh, and ring Roxette, or Daintree, or whatever she calls herself."

Mary smiled at Warren, aware that he was listening.

"Tell her we can do a deal. But no growing marijuana in the rainforest. I don't want trouble with the police."

Since Warren had shared a joint with Mike on more than one occasion, Mary knew the remark wouldn't seem surprising to him. Mary carried on,

"We won't need to come up here again to move the hives until the Wet."

John realized what Mary was saying. They weren't going to stage Mike's disappearance until the Wet.

"Fine," he said, "When is the Wet, again?"

"Hold on," said Mary as she spoke to Warren.

"Mike wants to know when to expect the wet season."

Warren shook his head.

"Hard to say these days with global warming. Last year we didn't have a proper wet season at all. We could be waiting another year. "

Mary spoke into the phone, "Warren said…"

John interrupted her.

"I heard," John hissed. "Does this mean we're going to have to keep Mike alive for another year?"

"Uh-huh," said Mary, "That's right. So we don't need to worry about anything right now. I'll be home soon, okay? 'Bye."

John hung up, muttering to himself.

Obviously, Mary didn't intend to stage Mike's disappearance before the Wet, meaning when he returned to Sydney, he still wouldn't have an ending for his book. He would have to wait until Mike was reported missing. And who knows when that was going to happen?

The man just wouldn't die.

John got into his car and headed for Sydney. All he could do now was wait.

CHAPTER TWENTY-NINE

As Mary drove south from the Daintree to her empty house, she realized that she just couldn't keep up the pretence of Mike being alive much longer.

Already, Matthew had called Mike's mobile several times and left text messages. Using Mike's phone, Mary had sent texts back.

The first said that he was fine and that he was more concerned for Mary.

The second advised Matthew that Valerie had refused to take custody of Rory's body and that he and Mary would have to bury Rory in Cairns. Unfortunately, (she wrote) the Covid restrictions meant they couldn't invite other mourners, not that there was anybody who would mourn Rory, anyway.

Both times there was an immediate call from Matthew to Mike's mobile, which Mary had ignored, followed by a text to Mike, then a call to Mary.

Mary had told Matthew that she thought Mike was grieving. Didn't want to talk to anyone. After all, she pointed out, and despite the circumstances, Rory was Mike's only brother and his last surviving relative.

"What about this cousin, John?" Matthew asked.

"Oh, he's been a great help," Mary said, honestly, "But now he's gone back to Sydney and Mike spends his time up in the Daintree, alone."

Matthew couldn't understand why his dad hadn't spoken to him; and Mary could hear the hurt in his voice.

She just couldn't keep this up. Even if she was still keeping Mike's death a secret from the rest of the world, she couldn't keep it from Matthew any longer. He had to be told, but how? Where on earth would she begin?

In the end, the problem solved itself.

As she drove up to the house, she saw a hire car parked in the driveway; and Matthew was leaning against it.

He straightened up and walked to the driver side of the campervan, surprised to see that it was Mary who was driving.

"Where's Dad?" he asked.

Now the time had come, Mary couldn't speak. Instead she just burst into tears.

Matthew pulled open the car door and practically lifted his mother out of the campervan and onto the ground.

"Mum, what is it?" he asked, wrapping his arms around her. "What is it?"

Mary's face was buried in Matthew's arms, which muffled her voice, but she still managed to blurt out,

"He's dead. He's dead."

"Dead?"

"Yes, dead!" Mary shouted.

Then the tears returned.

The last time Matthew had seen his mother cry was when his father announced that he had cancer and that he intended to cope with it himself, without bothering his family.

Mary had been heartbroken. She'd also been angry. *"How dare he push his family away? The people who love him?"* she'd said.

It seemed to Matthew that this was exactly what his mother had been doing recently.

"What's happened?" he asked, gently, and her anger

and grief overflowed.

"It was his own fault," she spat out. "He insisted on keeping bees. He didn't check if he was allergic to them."

Matthew doubted anybody would think to check if they were allergic to bees, but he was smart enough not to say so.

"Where's Dad now?" he asked instead.

"A crocodile's taken him," Mary wailed, leaving Matthew even more confused. It was obvious he wasn't going to get any sense out of his mother until he'd calmed her down a little.

"Let's get you inside," he said, and guided her towards the house.

Matthew sat Mary at the kitchen table.

"Would you like a cup of tea?" he asked.

"I'd rather have a scotch," she replied.

Matthew poured his mother a small scotch.

"Two fingers," she said, telling him to double the amount of the scotch, "And don't bother with water or ice."

Matthew half-filled the glass with scotch and handed it to his mother. She took a large gulp. Wiped away tears. Tried to smile.

"Remember when you were little?" she said, "Your dad asked you to give him two fingers of scotch and fill it up with water. You thought you measure the fingers lengthways, not sideways, and filled the whole glass with scotch with no room for water. Gee your dad was drunk that night."

Matthew smiled in sympathy with his mother, but he wasn't going to be distracted by family mythology.

"So, Dad was keeping these bees up in the Daintree, was he?" he asked.

"No," said Mary, "Here in the garden. He was trying to catch a swarm of bees here in the bush."

"So where was the crocodile?"

"In the Daintree," said Mary.

"I don't get it," said Matthew. "If Dad died here, what was he doing up in the Daintree?"

Mary took a deep breath.

"I took his body up there. It was days ago. The day Rory tried to kill him," she said.

"Dad's been dead for days, and you haven't told me?" Matthew almost shouted, although he hadn't intended to sound so harsh; he was just totally confused.

The effect was the same. Mary burst into tears again.

Matthew held his mother tight, waiting for her to re-gain composure, all the time trying to figure out what the hell had happened. His mother tried to explain between sobs.

"Your father was already dead when Rory tried to kill him. Your dad died first. Rory, or at least your Aunt Val-erie would have inherited everything, and she was in on the plan to murder Dad, and she accused him of being a paedophile."

Matthew held his mother at arm's length, and looked into her eyes.

"I'm not following," he said.

"She accused your father of being a paedophile, so that people would think he was depressed and shot himself. Then Rory was going to kill him"

"Shit! The bastard!" said Matthew. Then he corrected himself. "Pair of bastards!"

"I couldn't let him die with people thinking that about him," Mary pleaded.

"Of course not," said Matthew.

At last Matthew understood, at least the broad stroke of it, if not the details.

"So, you kept Dad's death a secret," he nodded. "But why didn't you tell me?"

"I couldn't," said Mary, "I couldn't involve you, in case anything went wrong."

"Mum," Matthew said, "If things had gone wrong and you'd ended up in goal, I'd have been involved anyway. Bad enough Dad dying. You being in goal would be impossible."

Mary again wiped her eyes.

"It might still happen," she said.

"Why?" Matthew asked, "Why haven't you told everyone a croc took him?"

"I was going to, today," said Mary, "I was going to leave the campervan up in the Daintree, with his beekeeping equipment around the place, then announce that he was missing. But the Park Ranger was there. He knows Dad. They were friends. He told me that we'd left the bee hives in a dangerous area frequented by crocodiles. He moved the beehives. Now we can't tell anybody your dad is missing."

"Why not?" Matthew frowned.

"Because he died from bee stings."

"If the body's missing, that doesn't matter, does it?" asked Matthew, "He could have been doing anything up there when the croc took him; fishing, boating…"

It was a light bulb moment for Mary. She wouldn't have to wait until the Wet. She could take the campervan back to the rainforest tomorrow.

There was still one problem.

"You're right," she said, "I'll take the campervan back as soon as you leave."

"I'm not leaving," said Matthew, "You need me. We take the campervan and the boat up to the Daintree tomorrow. Leave his phone by the riverbank. Then we come back here. You phone the Park Ranger and tell him I've arrived unexpectedly. Dad would want to see me but he isn't answering his phone. Could he go and tell Dad I'm here? That way somebody else finds he's missing."

Mary shook her head. She still didn't like the idea of Matthew being involved. She'd caused the problem. She should face the music alone if anything went wrong.

"Nothing will go wrong," Matthew assured her, "Besides, you can't get rid of me. I got into Queensland on compassionate grounds because Dad's had cancer. I have to self-isolate here for fourteen days. So, you're stuck with me."

Matthew wrapped his arms around Mary.

"Going up to the Daintree will be good," he said, "I'll be able to say goodbye to Dad in a place he loved. After that we can decide what we're going to do with this place."

He indicated the house they were standing in.

"I don't suppose you'll want to stay here on your own?"

"God no," said Mary, "Too many ghosts. We've only been here a couple of months and Rory has died in the shed. You father in the bush."

"Maybe we could all move to the farm?" said Matthew, "One thing the pandemic has shown me is that I can work from home, and home can be almost anywhere. There aren't many of us left in the family. We should all be together."

Mary clung to Matthew, liking the idea.

"'Course there's Uncle John. Or Cousin John, or whoever he is. I guess he's family too," said Matthew.

"I don't think he'll want to move to the farm with us,"

said Mary, thinking that if John ever appeared at the farm as John, it would cause all sorts of problems. "He's got his own life to live."

In truth, John wasn't feeling like he had much of a life to live at all, at the moment. He was in limbo. He couldn't finish his book, and until it was finished he was living on small stringer news pieces like the events at the horse abattoir in Queensland.

After visiting the farm and talking to Roxette, he had driven straight back to Sydney. He really had no further part in the plan. At least he fervently hoped he hadn't. All he could do was wait for somebody to announce that Mike was missing.

Not that he was expecting the news anytime soon, after his last chat with Mary, although he had started taking a keen interest in the weather reports, hoping for signs of an early wet season in Queensland. In the meantime, he returned to his usual routine, looking for stories and hanging about the pub.

One thing had changed, however. Covid restrictions were slowly being eased and Rugby League had returned to the small screen. No crowds at the stadium but it was live on TV. Even better, there were still restrictions on the number of people allowed in the pub. Fifty was supposedly the maximum but the four-metre rule, the rule that said the number of customers was limited to one for every four square metres of floor space, meant that in John's local there could only be a maximum of twenty-two people watching the football; he could enjoy the game, and his beer, in relative peace.

John pretty much kept himself to himself in the pub. Rarely speaking. Never raising his voice when he did. Tonight was no different. He sat alone in the corner, quietly watching the game. His beloved West Tigers were doing well and had gone into half-time with a useful lead. He was looking forward to the second half and got up from his seat, intending to get a new beer.

As he waited, standing back from the bar for his turn to order, he casually glanced up at the television, now playing the half-time Newsbreak.

He couldn't believe it. The message running across the bottom of the screen read:

Sydney man taken by crocodile.

"Quiet, everybody!" he yelled.

It was shock more than anything that caused everybody to stop talking. They'd never heard John yell before. They stared at him in amazement but he was oblivious to them all.

The Newsreader's voice was now clearly audible:

"A Sydney man who recently moved to Far North Queensland has been taken by a crocodile while fishing in the Daintree Forest," the newsreader said. *"The man who taught at a North Shore School prior to retirement was fishing alone at the time..."*

"Yes!" yelled John and held his arms aloft like a victorious gladiator. "Yes!"

He plonked his empty glass on the counter and headed for the door.

"Don't you want another?" the barmaid called after him.

"No," said John. "I've got to see my publisher."

THE END

CANCER, COVID, AND CROCODILES

BOOKS BY THIS AUTHOR

Big Fish To Rubber Ducky

A memoir about, among other things, a horse with a windy vagina, a three-year-old with a Strepsil addiction, a toe-biting possum and the time Mummy nearly drowned, and Uncle Martin made Daddy race him in a three-tonne steel houseboat down a fast-flowing river. For Kate, who was there but too young to remember.

The Parthian Shot

Liz Wright is set up by her husband of 20 years to take the rap for a crime he committed. She has a bold plan for revenge but she needs to win the cooperation of her fellow inmates: a narcissistic identity thief, an agoraphobic bully, a trainee nurse hoping for imminent parole and, trickiest of all, her husband's ex-mistress.

The Osmium Marbles

In the Australian Outback, a party of tourists souvenir eight odd-looking marbles from what seems to be the burnt-out wreck of a communications satellite. Only the CIA and ASIO have any idea that the marbles are more than mere space junk and they're not even letting each other in on what they know. By the time their various agents arrive at the site the marbles, and the tourists, have disappeared.

The invasion of Planet Earth has begun.

The Odyssey Of Rufus Jones

Alienated from his English family by the mystery surrounding his natural father, Rufus Jones escapes to a new life in Australia. But a minor misunderstanding with the Law lands him in jail where he struggles to survive until a chance viewing of the BBC series "The Human Planet" provides him with a guide to survival. A guide he finds even more useful on his release when he has to deal with murderous Bikies, pot-smoking Nymphs, and back-stabbing Politicians.

About The Author.

Ian Bradley is an award-winning screenwriter and television producer. He was central to the success of the international hit *Prisoner,* the classic heist series *The Great Bookie Robbery* and the socio-political drama *Embassy*, among many others around the world.

In Australia he was Head of Production for Kerry Packer and CEO of Crawford Productions. As Vice President of Drama for Grundy Worldwide he initiated long running drama serials in New Zealand, Italy, and Sweden.

Now retired from television he has continued creating, writing, and telling his stories. He likes working in a several genres. His first book is a humorous memoir; his second, an eco-refugee science fiction and his third, a heist novel set in a women's prison. His most recent novel, *"The Odyssey of Rufus Jones"* is a dark and funny political satire.

He lives in Sydney with his wife and editor, Anne Lucas, several kookaburras and a Blue Tongued Lizard named Adolf.